IN THE SHADOW
OF AN OBJECT
HYPERBOLE

by

Daniel Earl Harford

Published 2019 by Daniel Earl Harford

For contact information, please email:
danielearlharford@gmail.com

First Edition
ISBN: 978-0-578-48976-6

-For Pope Francis, and all of his children
—especially, our little Joey

"To the prophets wonder is a form of thinking."
                    -Rabbi Abraham Joshua Heschel

"...Meaninglessness is ontologically impossible..."
                    -Karl Rahner, S.J.

"The justice of God is the mercy of Christ."
                    -Pope John Paul II

"Preach
        the Gospel.

And
        if you must?

Use
        words."

        -Francis of Assisi

Prelude

"'Word by word, stone by stone, column by column.'
--First rule of reading, taken to be by some temple scribe,
Iraq, c. 4,000 B.C.E.

'Word by word, scroll by scroll, column by column.'
--First rule of reading, taken to be by some temple scribe,
Egypt, c. 3,000 B.C.E.

'Word by word, page by page, column by column.'
--First rule of reading, taken to be by some monastic scribe,
Italy, c. 900 C.E.

'Word by word, scroll by scroll, column by column.'
--First rule of reading, taken to be by some blogger, United
States, c. 2,000 C.E.

'Word by word, page by page, column by column.'
--First rule of reading, taken to be by some writer, United
States, c. 2,008 C.E."

"Here in this, one is free."
--First rule of reading, taken to be by some reader, United
States, c. 2,009 C.E.

PRIMUS

The man mused:
"Some drops of moon light

over a fiery rainbow

within a shadow."

And, the woman sang:
"Easy to chant when

over here so poetic*

in the moon, or sun."

"Aye, and my twelve days

of gift in Christmastide--with

snow? --keep the realm so

wealthy to a sun or moon.

Think not just one day of gifting! a disaster

economic--."

"What! was that the coming of an object hyperbolic

to this form? An horizon from over there so prosaic

toward the here and now so poetic, crying out a tale, lyrical?"

*(Note: Here on the folio sinister is the form poetic;

over there on the folio dexter is the form prosaic.)

I

"Are we playing out a mystery in the havoc of our times? Can any art--or beauty!--free us from oblivion? Meaninglessness?"

Meaning as it's understood is inherent in the shape of how the words are brought together as a whole. While the full significance in that shaping alters with every word that's used. Time alters the effect of each word on every other word; and every reading does the same through the core of meaning that's shaped by the writer. So, the outer horizon of meaning in that part of the poem over there reflects the inner horizon of an echo of some hyperobject in--.**

"I ask some rhetorical questions, and I get a lecture?"

There's nothing rhetorical about your questions, sir.

"No? I wonder if you've the wit to even duel with me."

Wit enough to know I don't know, until we do.

"So why even write, if you don't know?"

And that I'll never know, until I do the deed.

**(Note: Here on the right page is the form called prose;
  over there on the left page is the poetic form.)

—

SECONDUS

Later, the woman sang:
"Veil the sacred trust
across the firmament with
in a word alone.

Father!
        My father's
reign one day will end, and I
shall rule, poetic.

And none
            of the less
than perfect rhyme
                        will be allowed!
No peasant in soil,

nor dreg
                in sea, nor
child
        so poorly put to--."

    Interrupting, the man sang:
"Ages spent in passion

II

So now comes a duel within the sacred task of writing over time.

"Sacred task?"

Sacred task. I can't help wondering if writing isn't more a sacred trust than--.

"Reading? Next, you'll say that reading's sacred, too."

I don't know. Maybe. Maybe, it is.

"Why?"

For one thing, the ancient monastic tradition says it is just that. A sacred trust, and as much an action as the writing. When a word's read, do they not become one? One sacred act?

"Over a play on time to the space within the mind? Or on the page?"

Matching wits within a play of words. It's so ephemeral. If reading and writing are just mundane, why bother? Why? No, the sense of wonder in a word's true. It's true.

"The gap of death will come; and poetry will never rise."

—

for a word.

So play

so

much of love and life, woman.

One with man in timeless

touching now and then.

A mystery

one to an

other

when

in mystery found.

Lost one to an

other in

death, yet

found

be

yond some

mystery

of life and love

as one while still two.

Drops

of sky

soaking earth

and beauty

Poetry will come again.

"Never."

Never?

"Never, over here. Never seen. Falling into that gap of death, it is no more, even over there."

Why? Poetry, nevermore. Even over there in poetry. Why?

"There's the crux of it. In a question never answered."

Over here, is there any inherent meaning in the chanting of a teller in a tale? Why weave the threads into the tapestry of the story? Over there, why sing the poem into being?

"What can anyone offer? Elude a question with a question and get another. Or none. Or all. Now, awareness seems a better word to use. A better word to show how every word affects every other word within the weave of any tale."

Or in the harmony of a poem?

"Don't forget the gap."

Over here, what do we know about poetry? Over there. Well beyond the fixed wall of form, is the poet bound forever to his poem? His form? As we to ours. Never truly meeting.

in a woman forming
mist in man behind
a veil of life.
Reflecting.
Thinking.
Touch.
So love your father even
now within your angst."

    Woman:
"Softly timing touch
to touch unknown!
Soaring birds.
Whistling
air
that sings to earth from heaven.
Orisons tell of life.
A gift embracing
eternity.
My father
with his
way
has loosed a chaos
in our kingdom.

"An awareness, then, of never truly meeting? Look, one of the greatest breakthroughs in the understanding of the meaning of language was the awareness that the core within it was the sentence, not the word.   This is no question, but an awareness. One that leads to the thought--."

In the beginning was the sentence?

"Returning to your first idea, the meaning--."

Meaning as it's generally understood is inherent in the shape of how the sentences are brought together as a whole; while the significance of that shaping alters with every entrance into it.

"So time alters the effect of each sentence upon every other sentence. Every reading does the same through the core of meaning that's shaped by the writer."

That an outer horizon of meaning in a work reflects an inner horizon of a much more substantial meaningfulness, creating a significance over time.

"Are you saying works of art are compassionate by nature?"

Maybe, if by compassion you mean an awareness of the intense interdependence of all of art. Maybe. I don't know.

Gifting all

be free?

Fey!

A

movement

coming, too?

Woman or man, or

how reflect the heart

in

timing

human bridge

to briding come?

Betrothing, somehow,

love and bring the holy

one in two within our twain.

Touch

clearing

center, aye.

Yet, my mad

father rules

with a liberty."

   Man:

"From behind a cloud,

"So in the beginning was the sentence. Words echoing amongst themselves?"

A sentence is a relationship of words shaped together by a person.

"Who is a person because of his relationship with others."

Seemingly, the word reflects the person; the sentence, the family; the idea or stanza, the community; and on into the horizons along the edges of creation.

"The edges are chaos and death. But beyond is what?"

Or who.

"The center's a who we call holy. Metaphor! Why not go beyond the edge as well?"

Metaphor? Throughout the vast and intricate prism that is what it is, one facet expresses a reason for there even being poetry or art or prose at all in an ancient Nordic parable:

In all the years, Thor made a circle around the middleearth, trying to beat back the enemies of order and of life. He aged on year by year, and the circle of life and order and love withered.

I saw a light

pass away

afore

it

reached the earth, transforming

some mere mass of water

vapor into grace.

From horizon

toward now

an awe?

Dark

wonder at the trove

in parable

of the grail

within

me."

Woman:
"Truth!
Echo
on in love.
Life, fulfilling
holy passion plight."

"Dark

Then, Oden, the necromancer and lord of the fallen, strode out to the lord of trolls, snatched his arm and locked it firm. Roaring, he demanded, "Triumph will I, foul keeper, over this reek of chaos! The secret of the doing give me true, or keep your arm will I to scratch my back in Asgard until a ragnarok."

"Give to me your left eye," spat the troll, "and I will give to you in turn that precious secret true."

He released him, and gave up his eye, saying, "Tell me."

"The secret is to keep watch with both your eyes."

Some say that eye was the last sure hope of all the gods and humanity; and that against the chaos and darkness is only left the hammer of Thor--poetry and thought, not power. Others say--very little.

"And you, what do you say?"

My god is both beyond the edges of creation, and by his own action at the very center of my being. My words are an offering to his glory. But also, a way to witness to his involvement in us--before the bar of justice.

"The bar of justice?"

rose be

hinde the veil

of wedding joy

and ecstasy felt

for all in hope of yet

to be fulfilled eterne now."

"Dark

beaming

sunlight--wry

laughter coming

from some soaring bird."

"Within the love--in

love with Christ-

who is in

God: so

in

time to become so willing

that I reflect that light.

Yet from this holy

gift comes danger

as is shown

in Christ's

pain:

Yes, the bar of justice. You feel there's something sinister about it, don't you?

"Isn't there?"

How can there be something sinister about justice?

"And if it's broken, what then? Everything else is. You. Me. Everyone! Isn't it just a wicked weapon, masking itself underneath a simple word? No more than a mean tool of the wealthy and the powerful. It's a bent world, and so is this justice. That's sinister to me. What's it to you?"

Justice? Justice. Giving over to God his rights and due. To him? everything that is. To man? What he has given to him. To take from God what's his is injustice. To take from man what God has given to him is unjust. Justice isn't a mask, but an unveiling--.

"It's a shattered world! You know how you can tell a king? There isn't any crap on him. And why? His injustice masks as justice!"

Didn't the king of kings have the crap kicked out of him, when he was crucified? No, just because justice is bent and abused by men doesn't alter the love and truth of it, and its meaning. Taking away a right doesn't change the truth of it.

To be so clear in

love shall unmask

the sisters'

passion

true?"

"One

intent

on mating

frenzy--life comes

issuing from life--;

gift

from life

to life in

loving tone: Shade

the arc of being

one to one, two by two,

colors cascading in, out,

in,

out, too;

ecstatic

life enfolding

our beings to one."

"Why?"

Why?

"Yes, why. What are you trying to say?"

Now, that's a good question.

"Yes, it is."

Indeed.

"Well?"

It seems that all of the forms are inadequate.

"Inadequate?"

Yes, inadequate.

"Inadequate for what?"

To say what I want to say.

"So to say what you want to say, you have the gall to play with the great traditions of form. Play with the forms, and then expect the reader to take the time to understand."

Yes. And maybe even enjoy it.

———

TERTIUS

Man:

   "Heart in writhing

     bent toward

some

      pulsing effort

terse of nonviolently

  ellipsing

    embrace

  pulsing,

  throbbing,

  coming,

  encompassing in oneness

  won pivoting

  exposure

soul

  to

   soul to body:

    too

 soul: twin to two

  so loose in

time;

   taste so far, far!

III

"What is it that you want to say?"

That's very complicated.

"Simplify it for my simple mind."

Then, why write at all?

"Try."

Where to start.

"At the beginning?"

Or the end.

"At the end, then."

In the middle was the beginning in the end.

"What?"

See. Not so easy.

"Try to say it."

Humanity was made to love and worship God. That's simple enough. In the living out of it comes the complications. Those complications break through the forms, and deny them.

touch but once her body: soul

    mate (struggling

        to love

        [a cry

        between

        rainfall])

as words come to vary now

    with a dryness

that some

    how sings

        her to come in time."

"So you say."

So I say. Isn't that what you wanted?

"Yes.   Until you said it."

And once said, done. So there, the end within the middle, before the beginning.

"How formal."

And form is much more than just an ornamentation, too.

"So you say."

—

QUARTUS

22

Woman:
"or

shall I sing some

how of thought

or felt or

love,

touching into

a maelstrom yet

to come;

so

passion grasped

to another

corning!

Life

collapsing in

upon itself

in time

not

seen nor sighing

spatial depths

arcing

death

IV

"Wait a minute! Made for God? Where are you coming from?"

Forgive me. I do owe you that, don't I? For the sake of clarity, if for nothing else. I'm a Roman Catholic. Christ in the Eucharist is reality, itself. And, I love him.

"You're a real muddlehead, aren't you?"

You don't understand.

"Do you?"

Looking over there at that poem or over here to this prose, could you ever understand either if you didn't stand under the arc of meaning that's Christ for me?

"Are you trying to write a comedy?"

Or a tragedy in time. A critical element of a question asked along the edges of creation.

"What of the spatial relationships involved?"

Shape the various matrices one way and the meanings go along this curve; that way, along the other.

"Time?"

enthralling all
until he comes
for all

so

all might live in
his holy love.
Awake

my

heart, my soul, no
longer shaped in
marble

love

but gentle gift
in suffering
depth with

in

the sweeping arc
of covenant
given

you

to us in truth
full love and grace--."

Man:

Is a gift.

"You're using it like this as impressions wrought in love?"

Somehow crossing the organic barriers between poetry and prose, or poetry and music, song and prose. Probing the limits of possible form within form within form?

"or is poetry and the poet dead?"

Or worse yet, a dark force, a bad joke?

"'You remind me of that man,' the one monk said.

'What man?' The other asked.

'The man with the power.'

'What power?'

'The power of whom do.'

'Whom do?'

'You do.'

'I do?'

'Remind me of that man.'

'What. Man?'

   "Oh, my

Lord,

   still, I ponder

   woman's touching

   love so

dear

   within my heart

   and loins, and both

   pleading

truth

   in hoping now

   against all hope

   beyond."

'That man with the power.'

'That man with the power?'

'What? Power?'

'That power of whom do.'

'I do?'

'You do.'

'Do what?'

'Remind me of that man.'

Timing."

—

QUINTUS

Woman:
"Still

           I think

             and feel

    body

    mind

    soul

              still."

V

Timing? Comedy as a shrug and a glance, bonding the put-upon clown and the others around him in a singular empathy, and through a narrow fold in time reach a catharsis. To form an awareness of a common ground of being so wonderfully human that a laugh comes into time for a space is to touch the stars, the heart, the mind, and the soul--all at once. To know the poetics of time in the comic is a grace. Refined, it's to laugh in an echo of creation, musing.

"Timing."

—

SEXTUS

Man:
"Argent
    flow
        of
    light time
love to come as yet
      in ebony
for tide companions come
      to giving
ardent dawning or
surging tears
    in
love."

VI

Timing.

"The flaw that leads to the ending of the man:

'I have the thought, and it is good,' a man once said.

'But, I've the power, you see, and the will to use it against your thought and your good,' another said.

'How can you stand against the good?'
'Listen, goof, your good isn't my good. Your thoughts aren't my thoughts. Power conquers thought, and determines the good.'

End the man."

—

SEPTIMUS

32

Woman:

"Compassion

Spanning

One

another,

my love.

Sing

a heart in

to love?

Form

a seeking

after

this?

Struggle wry

again

a

loss again

a gain

so

daunting now

to once

in

VII

("Word by word, stone by stone, column by column."
> --First rule of reading, taken to be by some temple scribe,
> Iraq, c. 4,000 B.C.E.

"Word by word, scroll by scroll, column by column."
> --First rule of reading, taken to be by some temple scribe,
> Egypt, c. 3,000 B.C.E.

"Word by word, page by page, column by column."
> --First rule of reading, taken to be by some monastic scribe,
> Italy, c. 900 C.E.

"Word by word, scroll by scroll, column by column."
> --First rule of reading, taken to be by some blogger, United
> States, c. 2,000 C.E.

"Word by word, page by page, column by column."
> --First rule of reading, taken to be by some writer, United
> States, c. 2,008 C.E.)

Love: truth: beauty: kindness: compassion: patience: hope: courage: prudence: forgiveness: justice: mercy: gentleness: faith, interweaving one into the other to reflect the prisms of light in time to do an act of God within the commonweal of life.

to real love

arcing

one

to listen

clearly

now

upon some

one time

breast

of lover

twain or

plight

the troth trove

and fly

in

to mercy

and God's

love."

35

"What of the other side?"

The other side?

"Yes."

What do you mean?

"What of evil?"

Evil?

"And hate?"

Hate?

"And war?"

War?

"Yes. What of the other side of this life? What of the side where death awaits?"

—

OCTAVUS

Man:
"Still,
stillness reached: calmness come now
serenity, quiet poolness awaiting?
God
in loving woman's touching
fullness: Christ within all in all so loving
us
without us? still yet loving
all in all by compassion oft unseen some

seemly arc of consciousness; raising throughout
creation universal
love.
God parting the veil of his creation now
and being humbly so: Christ,
God
with us: Emmanuel to be crucified;
enthroned upon, beyond too
ken."

Woman:
"Do

VIII

Determination in a termination.

"What was that?"

The determination in the terminations. I was thinking about your story. About power shaping thoughts and ideas.

"And?"

The terminations were all such determined ventures.

"Triumphs of the will?"

Doubtless that. Appearing out of time to make a bar of soap out of a brother, and calling it doing justice.

"Justice. Doing justice? It's true, they believed they were doing good. But, doing justice?"

It cascades my thoughts over such a thoughtlessness.

"Wrathful justice taking vengeance comes to my mind."

Who of the myriads slain would be comforted by a bloody and ruthless vengeance? The angel of blood's a poetic truth. But man as the avenger of blood? Man's vengeance, never!

"An ugly word that one."

men understand womankind?

Or anything of mystery, or any woe?

Fey!

etched upon the very plaint

within our sex, we wonder stillness born

to

be under you and see to be

some feeling tear beyond the veil to blooding

there; hear, echoing in an undulant theme

of all in all a keening

red

through time a groan to touch a heart in dreadful

beat: Listen, listen, listen."

    Man:

"Wry

wisdom spent in wording real through time a scent

of prey: seeing, seeing,

pray?"

    Woman:

"Tell."

"Tell you what to be a man

Listen to the vibration of it as it shapes the soul around its meaning. Avenger of blood on a ruthless quest to spawn even more of a river, and call that justice. Shape that wrath around so delicate a thought as justice and feel the texture of it change into some appalling parody.

"Parody?"

A mystery (cascading thoughts [and evil has an horizon beyond all ken to fathom (yet still in time recalling that to God there isn't any mystery); but there's some sardonic twist, of course! in that parody of mystery that's called, evil] as only one), and maybe it's for the best to approach the whole of it for now in this way:

"Do you have any ideas?"   This man asked.

"You're asking me?"   That man answered.

"Yes, I am. Do you really think streaming a cascade of thought into a parallel story will work? Work any better in substance and form?"

"I don't know. A strange aside, if you ask me."

"I did ask."

"And I answered with an aside."

it is to be a man of honor bound in
time?
edge the struggle, woman! love."

"Go on a wheel in time. Await the saying."

"Time?
Time the echoes of my heart,
my darling."

      "Differences collective."
"Not differences collective. Difference
individual between."

"One."

"And the other one to be my only one."

"How is this to be so now?"
"Love."

"Wait."
    "What?"
        "Can you not feel it?"
            "Feel what?"

"Wait a minute, what was that?" This man asked.

"What was what?" That man answered.

"That."

"Where?"

"There."

"In the poem?"

"Yes."

"What do you mean?"

"I felt it," this man said.

"Felt what?" That man asked.

"Somehow, what we do is affecting it."

"Impossible."

"Nevertheless, we are."

"But, how?"

"I have no idea."

"Can you see what's going on?"

Woman:

"A change."

Man:

"What?"

"coming from there."

"Nay."

"Aye."

"Prose."

"Let me get closer," this man said, moving away.

"Be careful," that man said. "I hear those poets are crazy."

"'Mad, bad, and dangerous to know!' I will take care."

"You better!"

Silence.

"Do you see anything?" That man whispered. "What do I do if those loonies get their hands on him? Great idea this one."

—

NONUS

Woman:
"Not just prose to stay
in formal waters abrupt
a flower--."

Man:

        "Flowing. My lover,

        I see what in forming ken

        of saying, free prose--."

"Free prose breaks up
on the sacred ground due once
along to poetry."

        "So now form and rhythm,

        tone and chant have liberty

        within the language bent!"

                "Prose so free
of form thus now sweeps into our ordered realm in chaotic
weal, beloved."

"Weal of uncommon time in now,
and we would well, my love, be sure oft we do;

IX

Sound.

"Is that you?" That man asked.

This man stumbled over to him.

"What happened?"

"It was so strange."

"How strange?"

"The closer I got to the edge, the more time slowed and changed. Ideas took on forms, coming alive. Yet, there seemed more of a clarity for all of that. Even the shadows complemented the light."

"Did you go over into it?"

"No."

"Good. You were starting to sound poetic. That's all I'd need is for you to go over and become a poet. No wonder they're so crazy with all that aristocratic tripe. Form this and that!"

"Aut illic aut nullibi."

or not."

    Woman:

"You!

wax prosaic to a fault;

form turning to some vile plebeian

                        angst."

    Man:

"Angst?

       more like ennui!

What would you do if you were to do what you would do?"

"Do?

Do would I to cross over to heal the breach and fault,

                        would that I could I

                        so do."

"Asunder you would have us so

between this order and that chaos

met in here and there?"

                        "I do so now a mere

                        beginning toward that balm

                        to find; chaos writhes

"What did you say?" That man asked.

"Either there or nowhere," this man answered.

"What's that supposed to mean?"

"That depends on the language."

"In this one."

"Of course."

They were silent as the edges shifted in and out of a clarity; future tense transposed itself through that of past perfectly there and back again between the poetry and the prose.

"Well?" That man asked.

This man shrugged.

"Maybe, you've gone poet on me."

"Gone crazy, you mean?"

"Same thing."

"How would you know with all of this going on?"

Silence.

my soul in prosaic

dissonance."

Man:
"More the why I would
of you in this
disharmony?"

Woman:
"Gaze around you,
beloved!
Shards of poetic reality
wheel away from us–
sardonic mockery
of our muse.
All falling away
over there! too healing."

"Cruel."

"Cruel?"

"Aye."

"Nay!
Necessity."

"You aren't thinking of doing anything crazy, are you?" That man asked, shivering.

"Perchance, I am," this man answered.

"What? You can't do anything. What could you do? Go over there?"

"Attend to me. I must find out the why of it. Why this is happening. Over there the form is bending. Here? Here. Attend to my language and my voice! If it were to unravel, even break? Do you relish formlessness, and the abyss?"

"No."

"Well," this man said.

"What do you propose?" That man asked.

"Indeed."

"What?"

"To pass over there."

"How?"

"Just to do it is enough I feel."

"How do you think you'll do it?"

Man:
"Aye, how so it not to be

another way but this cruel

passing strange to lose you

thus upon this whirl of dire

wings of chance o'er there!"

Woman:
"Beloved."

"Harken once to me in this too

appalling margent,

and shall I then to your will

bow in deference and respect

for your high and noble dignity."

"Say on."

"In dread am I for your being's

sake to be so lost within

yon abysmal realm all

for naught."

"For naught?"

"Naught but for absurdity

This man answered, "The boundaries of my mind are as pliant as the edge of yonder poem and our prose, and I almost think it can be done. The one echoes the other, I think. If that is so, it can be done, and well."

A sound of wind now rising swiftly into a keening touch onto a falling away into a pulsing nothing still felt as something over there.

"See," he added.

"See what?" That man asked.

"The disharmony grows apace."

"And because of that, you'd chance your only sacrifice?"

"Would you?"

"Hardly."

"So."

"Fool."

"Maybe, so."

"If you do it well, I want to know the why of it. So come back."

52

and passion plaint
within your sacrifice."

Woman:
"Nay, my love.
For you and all
within this plane
do I cross o'er
that line of woe."

Man:
"Cruelty."

"Nobility!"

"Aye. "

"Did you feel that?"

"Nay."

"I must away o'er there."

"Mayhap?"

"Aye?"

"Do return else my honor

"If, I can," this man said, moving away. "Watch for any thing passing back over after me."

"Farewell," that man said as he passed from his sight. Faintly, he heard, "And you."

Then, void.

Sometime beyond the stars, an ylem came and went into a nothingness untold by one who failed to see the light.

Something there.

Anything here.

Anything there.

Something here.

Nothing there.

Nothing here.

Nothing.

No one.

Some one.

Someone.

and my good name do die
together with you;
and then do I for allowing
you this quest
along."

                    Woman:
                    "Nay, my love! we be
                    as one either here
                    or there."

     Man:
"True."

                    "As to why I go and not
                    you so well you fathom.
                    What strength in me
                    to hold this realm?
                    Your honor is as mine,
                    and name as one."

"Remember well, then."

                    "Aye. Farewell!"

That man?

That man.

"Is anyone there?"

Silence.

"Is anyone else there?"

Silence.

"Here! Is anyone else here?"

Silence.

"I don't care. Here or there, are you?"

"Aye," a voice came from the edge, faintly.

"A woman?" He whispered.

"Where are you?"

Over a rising wind, he called out, "Who are you?"

"I have no idea," the voice answered. "Who and where are you?"

"Over here."

—

DECIMUS

Man, oft the younger:
"Fey,
dread
        the coming
                not to be
limbs of mellow basking arc;
                        in light
                                of moon
too
orison mare mar
                winds
of timeless
            now
            and
                when
                    to be so
                            passing
strange,
or
    tearing of a god
                    in
mortal quest.

X

Another wind came into the
first, rising sharply with it and
then falling into naught.

"No idea have I of who I may
so be," the woman said, coming
into view. "How so is this to be
so within and out of time?"

He gasped.

She stumbled into his arms.

"I don't know," he said.

"Who are you?"

They released each other.

"I don't know," he answered,
slowly. "Some call me, that
man."

"What is your name?" She
asked, shivering into another
little wind.

A knight was riding down a path
one day, and spied a little bird
upon
his way. It had the wings spread
flat beside it and the feet stuck
toward the sky.

Going neither left nor right
around, he stopped and stared
and asked, "Hoy, little one,
pray tell me what it is you do
to hazard so my tread and pace
upon you?"

"I heard the sky would fall,
today," the bird piped up.

"So?"

"Your point of question being?"

Shards of fate transfiguring?

                too

blood

    the tears through veils

        unseen

          nor felt in

            time

to time

    to

      be

        one

         to

          one.

Be

muse

    to wit

      bemusing

        bitter blending sweet

of love

    beyond

      an arcing

wit.

Less

    to

"I don't know!" He said.

"Neither do I," she said.

"Scent so fragrant."

"Do I call you, that man?"

"Some do."

"That man."

"Yes?"

"No. I wished to touch the
sound of it."

"I see."

"Do you?"

"Do I what?"

"Know the why of here."

"The don said it was the free
verse over there."

"Free verse?"

"Why are you resting so upon
the path before me?"

"I shall try to hold the sky up,
when it falls."

"You plan to hold up the
vastness of the sky with those
two puny limbs?"

"Yes, I do."

"Absurd is that beyond all
words to tell, droll fool."

"Do you think?"

"Assuredly so."

"Well, even so, one can only
do what one can do."

And so failed the tale without
a knowing here or there. Did
the sky
fall? If not, how long before
the bird grasped it had been
misinformed?

                more

                         in

                              honor

                                   bent

                                        onto

                                             highest

reach, and then

                    to

                         fall, witless?

fey!"

(Void:

some time yond the stars,

ylem came and went into

nothingness untold.

     Someone there?

     Nothing there?

     Nothing.

     Nothing here?

     Someone here.)

    Man, oft the younger:

"Over there?" She asked.

"Over there," he said.

"Not here?"

"Here?"

"Here."

"Why here?"

"There is it not to be as source of wrongness be."

"You jest," he said.

"Jest?" She asked.

"Jest."

"Why jest?"

"The wrongness can't be here."

"And why not?"

"Here, all is true."

"And so would say a poet."

Blind in one way, insightful in another, was it simply hungry when it moved? Or did the sky fall truly in that world with talking birds? In the judgement of the knight, braving the fall like that was to be absurdity, itself. While to another passing knight, that one might seem even more absurd in talking to a bird. In that one's eyes not at least to try one's best against a hopeless situation was the meaning of despair, rather than the situation, itself. So, it saw the knight as the one who was absurd. In the bitterness of that kind of humor (with a

"Yonder ground did mark

and move the very base

of time.

      Is anyone

there?"

(Chaos.

      Order.

            Chaos.

                  Order.

                        Chaos.

Order.)

                        Man, oft the older:

                        "Yes.

                        Am I?

                        yes."

      Oft the younger man:

"Who

            are

                  you?"

"Woman, you sound like one
of them from over there," he
said.

"Are you benighted?" She
asked.

"Benighted?"

"In shadowed shards of
darkness, you try to see me.
You try to see your self as a
center fixed. So you see me
moving around you, and not
my own self. Our center is
more than we are, or were, or
ever could be so."

"Poet!"

"In bitterness you say so.
Why?"

"I love you. Yes! I love you,
and I can't at all say why I do."

root within despair) is found
the failure of the tale. The
little one's
words ended with a wryness
wrung from wrath, rather
than a courage calling down
the other into some solidarity.

"'Well, even so, one can only
do what one can do.'"

It fell over.

"Listen: Once there was this
very old monk who lived
alone in the waste. He prayed.
He worked. He fasted.
He prayed the Psalms. He
worked by weaving baskets,
selling them in a market. Of
what little
he earned, he gave most as
alms. So, he fasted more."

"One night, two young monks

Oft the older man:
"Whom.

      Where am

            I?"

Oft the younger man:
"Here."
"Not there?"
"Here.

      Prose the free

         reigns,

            and pulls all

apart."

"I see.
What do you do about what to do?"

"Nothing.
What can I do about what to do?"

"And so chaos."

"So chaos seems to be so, old one."

"Free prose, you say?"

"You love me," she said.

"Yes," he said.

"So."

"So? You're a poet, and aristocrat."

"So?"

"And I'm a worker."

"So?"

"How could you ever love me?"

"Are you a peasant, too?"

"As well."

"Bittersweet."

"Bitter, sweet?"

"So. I love you, too."

"Sweet bitterness!"

"Aye."

came to the door of his cell and asked for a word from him."

"In silence, he washed their feet. Prepared a meal for them with all he had to give. Then, as they ate their fill, he sang a song of the king to set them at their ease. He cleaned up quickly after they had finished; then sat down with them in silence."

"Soon the arc of passing troubled one of his guests enough for him to say, 'Give a word, abba. Why belabor time?'"

"The old one was silent."

"'This old fool has no word for me! Stay if you will; I shake away his

Oft the younger man:

"Aye, coming from over there."

Oft the older man:

"Let me ponder.

       Perhaps to shape it like a wind

in form

and move the pulsing sway,

          word

            and sign onto some

pure stability?"

"Aye!"

Time fluttered along the edges of folding space within the form of a wind unseen by either of them.

"You love me?" He asked.

"Aye," she answered. "And you love me."

"Yes, I do."

"Yes? Aye. 'Tis but a harsh and dreadful thing to love in time. Beloved.

dust from me!' The young man cried, and fled alone into the waste."

"'Why did you stay?' The old monk asked."

"'Your word was in your acts of love,' he answered. 'Why were you silent?'"

"'A stone only hears a silence in the hardness.'"

Quite the mystery.

—

UNDECIMUS

Oft the younger man:
"With understanding
in humility unseen:
Whirlwind moving out

and in
                desert dust
reflecting water sounding,
sifting life in time

beyond
            all playing
mystery
              in a lave wave
of whispering sighs;
or
        of swirling ice:
crystals miming
                          rain swept seas
Man   woman
            and   love.
Yet,

XI

Across the waste of form was
silence for a moment.

"We love, and we don't even
know our names," he said.
"How can that be?"

"Perchance love goes beyond
a mere name," she said. "Even
so, I shall call you, Sans."

"Sans?"

"Sans."

"Sans."

Silence with an echo far away.

"Then, you'll be an Antigone
to me," he said.

"Antigone?" She asked.

"Antigone."

"A mystery, you say?"

Or a sensus plenior? Defined
by one venerable Catholic
theologian as the deeper
meaning, intended by God
but not clearly intended by the
human author, that's seen to
exist in the words of Scripture
when they're studied in the
light of further revelation
or of development in the
understanding of revelation.
In this, even the minor
points, such as whether the
human authors were aware of
any divine intention beyond
their feel or not of it, are in
dispute. Still, there seems to
be enough of a

how close are we?
Skin to skin

        in passion spent?
Rising sunset glow
on lips

      of softness
touch to softness finding some
beauty as a bird?"

  Oft the older man:
"Inotherwords, hope.
From out that earth in the heart
yond the inn of mind

impressions

        coming
through in waves: atonal voice
echoing now and then.

Still
    only
        a verse
expression

The wind anechoed.

"See, poetry," she said.

"Poetry?" He asked. "Do you
not see the very truth within
a name?"

"No matter what your name,
you'd smell as sweet and
bitter."

"Truth has always been the
most poetic of forms in life."

"How so, here?"

"If truth be here, then poetry
be both there, and here."

"Poetry."

"Am I not an Antigone
conceived once more?"

"Are you tragic, then?"

consensus to make of it, at
least, a viable thought in any
truth worthy of that name. So
in Scripture the Lord could
write both large and small
beneath the writing of the
merely human. But to us, the
written revelation is sealed.
The sensus plenior, if granted
to Scripture, will not reach
into the mere profanity of art
and poetry.

"Profanity?"

Profane and profane, catholic
and Catholic: The meanings
of the words
are always expanding or
contracting.

"Breathing?"

Breathing.

      of

            impressions
felt in depth: Oceans
of
      humankind
            that
reaches far,
        one to one,
                one
to all
      winding
         moors."

   Oft the younger man:
"Humble
       creature
           now
to listen:
       Simple work
             in
simple life (forest

moving
       glade

"Not now," Antigone said. "With you."

Sans scratched his head, and said, "That yet calls to be fore seen."

"You see, poetic."

Another sound arose with strength renewed, and fell away again, but with an echo of another something.

Or, someone?

"What was that?" He asked.

"What was what?" She asked, looking around.

Echo.

"That," he said.

"Quiet," she whispered.

Another one.

"Profane, and sacred?"

Yes, the sacred, and profane.

"At one time didn't that profanity mean all that wasn't sacred?"

Now, isn't that word flattened to a coarsened stump? As is the other one.

"Both down into a common and tattered sense of time in meaning."

Or take catholic and Catholic.

"One meaning simply the universal. The other--."

Meaning more than all the words could speak in--.

"That's absurd."

     in time),
clatter of dish on dish, glass
not breaking sound (trees

echoing the crack
of seedlings cry), hands touching
metal cold in search
of

    oppression
       seen
in power and profit (sea
overwhelming mountain

and

    magma
       rising
from the center
         of
           the
             earth);
still, returning good
for

Faintly, a voice called,
"Hello."

"Hear that?" He asked.

"Quiet," she whispered.

Other changes flowed over
their common senses as they
held each other close.

"Aye," Antigone blew into his
ear. "'Tis another farther over
there."

"Changing all," he said.

"'Tis so."

"'Tis?"

"'Tis! Changing all."

"Hello," the voice said, much
closer now.

"Can you make out who it is
yet?" She asked.

Not being able to use the
one for the other's a deep
constraint not because of a
limitation of understanding
on the part of the reader,
but rather because every
word affects every other
in the language. But with
the understanding that
the sentence is the core
of meaning, anyone can
uncommonly sense that
maybe every sentence affects
every other one that was, or is,
or will be!

"You're beginning to really
sound pedantic, fool."

That's disappointing.

"Irritating is what I call it."

So much for using that kind
of clown as a voice.

evil

(gnarled,

withered

branch,

soaking

eons

within

a pond;

wood

hue

naught

in

shades

of

water

clear and caught?

showing

rich,

green,

green plants; a bird flies

on

to

one:

"No," he answered.

"Is anyone there?" The voice cried out more clearly and closer still.

"Aye!" She called. "Over here!"

"That tears it, sweet," Sans whispered.

"Tears it?"

"Is that voice a friend, or is it a foe?"

"I think it another man, at least."

"Then, a foe."

"How so?"

"To me."

"So."

"So?"

"or like this effect?"

What effect?

"Using the language like this to tell a story? The effect's like a series of quick commercials. But all of them are bound so tightly together. It's building in intensity. Until, what?"

Concinnity.

"A what?"

A concinnity.

"Define it."

Wouldn't that be pedantic?

"Try."

An intense harmony?

"Are you asking me?"

No. Peek in the book.

             mirror)!
Trust on, trust on, still, under
withering times (dove

in waves of motion)
where (leaflets sensing the roots
of forests) the all
of
        man
                kind
                        in
                                to
children dying ugly on
to a war (loess

and wind);

                chaotic
depths
        sown
                in
                        strife

"Greetings, fair one," the other man said as he came up to them, bowing gracefully to her.

"Are you a poet over here?" She asked, and smiled.

Sans glared at him.

"Who me?" The other asked, scratching his head.

"Aye, you," she said.

"Dear lady, never so."

"Never?"

"Never."

"Why?"

"Do you not know the why of it?"

"Know the why of what?"

"Clown!"

I can only hope to be one.

"You're serious."

Why wouldn't I be?

"Don't you want to be a tragic figure?"

Aren't they much the same?

"You're kidding me."

See, comic.

"But, they're not the same!"

No?

"No!"

Why not?

"They're just not."
Hear a laugh. See a tear.

"See a tear. Feel a laugh?"

deriding

kith and kin as one

will

to

peace

a

way

come

such

as

be

as not to

be

in

sun

set

sin;

and

rain

fall

(a

core

sound)

"The poet must be dead," the stranger said.

"Dead?" She asked.

"Dead."

"Here?"

"Aye, here."

"And there?"

"Maybe. 'Tis here we are, not there."

"'Tis true."

"Or maybe not, my lady."

"Thank you for that, kind sir."

"Nothing at all. Dare I say that as to poets, that honor have I never known."

"So be it."

Silence.

That's it.

"Fool."

How quaint. No fool in a republic. No king, or court. No comedy. And no tragedy-- in a republic.

"So, the poet's dead."

A tale thrice told to many with another one about how God is dead.

"All with a harmony in some tritonal sway?"

One way or another, this brings to mind a tale within a tale about a dead poet.

"Very well, tell me, if you must."

Many moons ago, I was unceremoniously invited

                to

                        educe

                                some

                                        coming

whirlwind reign in time?

Cry

        less

                sound

                        in

                                to

any night of wraithful wrath

in human folly.

(The moon is clear some

where.) Humility points to

(Both sun and moon light

interlacing

                with

in) contrasting omissions

Sans cleared his throat, and said, "Don't you know a poet when you see one?"

The other man looked at him for a moment longer than was needed. Then, still staring at him, he asked her, "A poet, are you?"

"He thinks I am," she answered.

"I would not be at all surprised, if you were. Marred and blurred upon your edge, you may well be so. But for all of that, you are true and highly born! What do you in so waste a land such as this7 To be sure, it must be a task both

for a short visit to a little house of nonviolent love (I had been told before I went, and was after told again, a sign sat in Latin above the door. Translated into English, it read, "Do not let the illegitimate get you down." I never saw it, really. I only saw the people, not the things).

On the first night, Phil--of most happy memory-was being questioned by a reporter from West Germany. Later, after that, he was leaving to take her to the airport, and I, being me, asked him, "Mind if I go along with you on your trek?"

rueful plaint (shadowed
flowers

       weaving

          in

colors

       wavering
          flow
             some
song); archaic center
holding

       tender
          love
in
   action
     true

well and honorably borne.
Perchance, your humble
servant might assist you fair?"

Antigone sighed. "I forget
the why of me, you see. I
know not here or there of me.
If only I could remember!
A doing and a message? A
mission and a pledge? An
order and an honor?" She
sighed, again. "I forget."

Moving closer to her, the
other said, "Come here to me,
fair child. Let me shield you
in my arms, and stroke awake
your sleeping memories."

The wind stirred.

Then, it passed away.

He looked at her and then at
me, saying, "You're that poet
from Florida, aren't you?" He
shrugged into my nod. "Why
not?"

On the ride, the talk was
small but also keen of both
the holy and mundane. Of
that, I can recall just mostly
Phil and her. He asked of
her of her land; she of him of
ours.

Then from the back, I asked,
"Who do you think was the
greatest German who ever
lived?"

He glanced at me through the
rearview mirror and raised an
eyebrow.

Worlds of meaning in that
mere eyebrow as he coughed
away a laugh.

                    and

                        just

                            in

time

    (as

        a

            small

                bird

will

    in

        a

            morning,

a

    dawn

        on

            to

                dusk);

                    stillness

wanes another thrust

to

Sans moved in between them,
and pushed the other back,
saying, "Unhand her, villain!"

"You dare touch me so?" The
man said as his hand rested
on the hilt of his sword.

"How dare I not?"

"Ah." Then, more to her but
still not taking his eyes off
that man, the stranger said,
"Not so this, a worker, to
so dishonor me with such a
slight thing as a touch. Dare
I stand such an unheard of
happening, and not give out a
blooding?"

"Yes! A worker am I, and
proud to be one. Try to think
for once, you fop!"

"Schiller (writing to a friend
about what was happening,
in at least his own mind,
while creating a poem 'the
intellect has withdrawn its
watchers from the gates,
and the ideas rush in pell-
mell, and only then does the
[creative (polysemy when
used with Scripture as meant
by the sensus plenior can be
tentatively granted for the
sake of this wave of thought, I
hope: So that I can delve into
how Dante wanted his poem
to be taken by della Scala.
I read in it that the poet is
using a traditional exegesis
of a psalm as an example of
how to read his work. In other
writings,

plan

     and

       play

         wry
(and the willow only seems
to weep) past arranged?"

  Oft the younger man:
"The now? a future
rooting in the branching stem
of historical

vent

    and

      bent.

       Nature
into pulsing forms, reaching
human quality?

Man

    thinks.

"Ho!" The stranger said. "'Tis one beyond his place and ken."

"I'll show you the meaning of my grasp, and a better way!" Sans said.

"You wish it so?"

"Be plain."

The other threw down his gloves between them.

"What's this?" Sans asked, spitting.

"I challenge you to a duel of honor."

"Say what?"

"A duel of honor, and for the sake of the lady."

"Child."

"Fool."

he even says that all the many profane works are intimately woven together. He, at least, draws the holy over the canon walls into the thick of the mundane. Yet, he was an avowed Thomist; so he wasn't espousing some neo-pagan synthesis, was he? I think Dante meant two things at the core of his critique. First, the closing of the scriptural canon was to limit us, not God. Second, a poet has an awareness of his work, not unlike that of God's own in relation to his written word. He saw an implicit meaning and a metaphor in it on the poet's mind reaching out to the other) mind] review and

                Woman

                           thinks.

Think
          on
                   it
                        in
                             moon
                                   light
                                          through
echoes dancing form

to

     life

          to
               be
                    so
     great
          and
               vast

The ground rippled slightly
under them.

The wind rose and fell away,
again.

The horizon moved, and a
little growth emerged within
the desert of the place.

"Coward," the courtly one
said with a sneer.

"Walking waste of time!"
Sans said, stepping up to him.

Antigone came between
them, saying, "Men!"

They both stepped back in
surprise.

The stranger gasped.

"Woman!" Sans cried out.
"What are you doing?"

inspect the multitude)."

Her flight was on time.

The silence was good on the
ride back, but I had to repeat
her choice again out loud.

"Says a lot," Phil said.

"Yes, it does," I said.

It began to rain.

I lit another cigarette and
coughed.

Then silence again, but for the
traffic and the rain.

"To think and choose a poet,"
I said. "A poet?"

"Yes, a poet," Phil said.

"Can't think of many here,
who'd choose a Berrigan."

A

    tree

      of

       life

as

  one

   to

    all

     in

one

  hug

   from

     God

      in

Christ;

  a

   fire

    a

     round

      a

       heart

"You, an egotistical snob with pretentions to wit," she said, facing the one; then, turning fully on the other, continued on, "And you. You say, you love me? But you only stroke your ego with your pride and his!"

"Forgive me, love," Sans said, touching her face. Then, nodding slightly once, he said to the other, "Your pardon, sir, I misspoke."

"Too rude for wit," he said more to himself, adding, "Maybe it's this world around us that's doing it to us." Then said with a bow, "No, sir, no! pardon me. I it was who misspoke."

"Or an Eliot?" Phil asked with a laugh.

"Would that some could say your brother," I said.

"would you?"

"I could."

"Don't. You'd only embarrass yourself--."

"Embarras du choix."

"And him."

"Not any more than our placing him with that poor expatriate. Maybe, we're all exiles."

"Prophets. Or not."

"So, we're left with only generals. Not one king among them."

"There are the clowns."

alive and alike

as

        tectonic

                        plates

a moving wave, stilling time

to a time too much.

Inside as in out

of the very time to be

one to one as birds

fly,

    some

           how,

              south

                  ward

formal in a spring tide rain."

   Oft the older man:

"Web of being, son,

"Honored," Sans said. "Might we know your name?"

"Parsafal," the other said. "And yours?"

He gazed at her for a moment, and then answered, "Some call me, Sans."

"You have declared your love for this fair one?"

"As she has for me."

"Aye? 'Tis so, my lady?"

"Aye, 'tis so," she said. "I forgot. I've forgotten so much in this world here from over there, I just forgot again my love."

It began to rain.

"I even forgot I thirst!" She continued on, looking oddly at the rain.

"Clowns as bitter and dark as the generals," I said.

Laughing, Phil asked, "Aren't the generals our clowns?"

The humidity had put out the cigarette, and I placed it in the ashtray.

The rain eased.

"Clowning against the clowns, then are we?" I asked as we pulled up before the house.

"Maybe so," Phil said as we got out of the car.

"One does what one can."

"One does what one ought to do."

The rain stopped.

my

   son.

     Quite

        the

           blow

was

     that

       one

         passing

           wind

               so

dark in telling strange

too."

    Oft the younger man:

      "Slackening,

           now,

I

  think."

"This mist isn't going to help us much," Sans said.

"I have some Benedictine in my scrip," Parsafal said, reaching into it and pulling out a flask.

She took it, and drank some; then, gasping, she handed it to Sans who did the same. He offered it back to her. With another sip, she wiped her lips, and gave it to the knight.

Parsafal took a long tilt of it. Then, put it away.

"Thank you," she said.

"Indeed, thank you!" Sans said.

"I saw an oasis back over here in passing strange," Parsafal said, pointing

As we were walking up to the house, he slapped me on the shoulder, saying, "Clowns." He laughed. "Good one, kid!"

Remembering how we had walked into the house, I think how quaint the idea that a poet like a Dante or a Schiller would be a puppet of any reader, any where or in any time. Even of each other. Quaint. If that. Because after deconstructing everything into an unsightly pool of words, why couldn't any reader rework any string of words into an other thing unknown to any writer, now or then or yet to be?

"Some think so."

Oft the older man:

    "Chilling

        to

          the

            bones!

But

   stars

     of

      tone

       tide

in

  to

   a

    trough

     so

    calming

     for a moment

        true

across the waste. "It had
a goodly pond with fish, I
think. Some trees of nut and
fruit as well. Shall we go or
no?"

"Aye," she said.

"Lead on, my friend!" Sans
said.

They followed him into the
mist.

"How far is it?" She asked.

"Not far," the knight
answered.

All they could hear were their
footsteps in the quiet.

And maybe the breathing,
too.

"Wait," she said.

I think not.

"Then does the writer reign?"

A man went into a bar far, far
away one day. He sighed as he
got a drink, sat and drank it
down.

The barkeep raised an
eyebrow as a question.

Nodding, the man looked
around as he filled his glass.

Another man walked in to sit
at the bar.

The barkeep gave him a beer.

He drank it down in one
smooth motion.

The eyebrow raised.

as time to space in

space

     through

        time

             to

               be

of once or twice or thrice too

of sorrow--of woe!"

   Oft the younger man:

"Woe. And. Sorrow?

Wry in thoughtful horizons,

inner and outer,

spent

     or

        not

            the

               drift

to catch the roe in timing

beyond the present."

   Oft the older man:

"What is it?" Both men asked at once.

"I need to rest," she answered.

"Let me carry you," Sans said, taking her up into his arms.

She squealed in laughter.

"Good man!" Parsafal said. "Let us go on."

So, they did.

The wind began to blow against them, rising steadily.

The mist fled.

Slower and slower still, they pressed forward against it.

Step by step by step.

"I think not," he said, and disappeared.

"Who was that?" The man asked.

"Rene Descartes," the other answered.

I like to think there was a laugh.

"Maybe. Always, if the writer had his way."

Of course! But in a place where the writer ruled supreme, wouldn't the reader be but a commodity? A thing to be manipulated? Sold? Bought? A tool of the trade, so to speak?

"An instrument of the god who writes?"

The mere tool of the gods!

"All

    foot

        steps

           in

              life

go

    one

        by

           one,

              too; by two

seas apart from one

to

    one

        of

           two

              by

two,

    not three

        by three,

           but

              two

by

    two

        to

Step by step.

By step.

"Put me down!" Antigone cried out over the almost endless sound. "Sans, put me down, now!"

He placed her gently on the ground. His hands trembling from the passing strain, he sat down beside her.

Parsafal gazed down at them, fighting the wind. Then, he sat down, too.

The wind screamed.

They moved closer to each other.

The wind eased; and then the sound into a very fragile silence fell.

"Getting a little rusty, too."

Not funny.

"No?"

No! In a world created in such a way, the little godlet comes to strut and sway across his talent and his stage. No giving here, only taking. A self-sustaining genius caught in worship of itself. Havoc strewn along the pathway of the course. Truth? a tattered remnant of what it might have been in some other world in kindness wrought, and not in bitter pride! Hope? What hope? in the realm of the divine poet where the lowly reader is but a

       get

           one,

or

   two

      or

        three

          or

more

    in kind

      to be

         as

           one

of time beyond the now.

See

   the

      wing

        of

          living

ebb; wing in flow of being

true to forming light

of moons in ages

past a time of solar winds

"How are you?" Both men asked her at the same time.

They laughed.

"Well, hungry," she answered.

"I have a touch of the Benedictine left for you," Parsafal said, taking out the flask and handing it to her.

She finished the liqueur; nodded and smiled her thankfulness before returning the flask with the question, "How far?"

"Not far. Just over that rise, I think."

"I think I can walk it."

They helped her stand up.

creature to be used to feed that pit of pride. And in that place where the poet's the one and only be all in all, where is love? It isn't there!

"Is it in a joke too far? In a bleeding tear? Or in the touching hand? Love? Your image of that godless godlet's sway is an idea. Still, an idea's just a complex thought, isn't it? A poet's simply a poet, isn't he? If more than that, he's bent into a dark and unholy ideal. An idea can die, and even be mourned by some who ought to know better. Or not by those who ought to have struggled to keep it alive. A man's mourned, or not."

adust a never

when

    or

        where

            or why

to find a wren within some

bit of sky or rain

with

    out

        a

          single

star

    or rhyme

        or reason

            come

now and then a knot."

   Oft the younger man:
"Ought

    to

      be

        a naught

or comma

"I can carry you," Sans said.

"No, I can do it, love," she said.

"Good, I'm hungry, too."

"Onward," Parsafal said, leading the way.

Soon, they topped the rise, and saw an idyllic oasis. Stumbling to the edge of the water, they drank their fill. Then, they ate some fruit and nuts. Antigone and Sans played in the water; while, Parsafal pulled out a line and fished. He caught some of them, built a fire and cooked them. They ate, until satisfied. And sighing, rested.

But, an idea's on a different plane of existence from a man, isn't it?

"As far as I can grasp the core of the fighting between the three waves of reasoning, it's on an order of magnitude, and about a dynamic struggle between precedence, power and priority. The--."

And you say, I'm the poor, pedantic clown.

"If you please, I was speaking."

Rude of me. Sorry.

"It was nothing. You're forgiven. Now, where was I--?"

I don't know.

tracing

    here

        or

there,

  now

    and then,

        too."

Oft the older man:
"My

  son,

    my

      son, heed

to me

  and a tale

    to tell

you true horizons

long

  from

    here

      to there,

now or then or may well be."

Oft the younger man:

The silence was a balm to
their souls.

Soon, they slept.

When Antigone awakened,
she found the men sitting
together, gazing at her with
smiles on their faces. "What?"
She asked, sitting up too
quickly and groaning, "My
head."

The smiles faded away.

Sans took her hand and held
it, gently.

"Are you feeling poorly?"
Parsafal asked.

"My head hurts," she said,
cupping it in her hands. "No
more of that fire for me.
Understand? None!"

"Witless wit."

At least, I've the wit to recall
what my thoughts had been
before the question.

"As if they were worth a
memory. Idea's truth to the
idealist. The ideas take both
priority and precedence.
With an order of magnitude
granting an autonomous
power to those ideas, and
a determined unreality to
the whole of living man and
woman. The materialist? Put
simply, a body should place
a diaper on its head, because
ideas are just organic ooz
coming out of the brain at
times. A realist sees both
body and mind as true. Ideas
are derivative. A fruit of both.
Or nothing."

"So. Tell of a tusk.

A teak? Or a whale.
Simple and solid, and true.
Beautiful, graceful

in

    all that

        you say,

you struggle in all that you do in time."

    Oft the older man:

            "sunrise

you are

      to

        my sunset.
Say you see

       it, my son,

           light
of my life; and grief

as with

      any

        one

"Try jumping into the water,"
Parsafal said. "I've enough
fish for breaking our fast. Go.
Do it."

"Go," Sans said, standing and
helping her up. "You will feel
better. Trust me."

She did.

The men laughed at her cry
at the shock of finding out
how cold the water felt at the
moment she entered it.

"Are you mocking me?" She
cried out, jumping up and
down.

"How's your head feeling?"
Sans asked.

"Mockery!"

Deriving?

"Look, isn't the writer relating
to his reader like a husband to
his wife?
Not meaning any mystical
intimacy, but a bond of trust
and solidarity. Inotherwords,
the writer and the reader
almost co-create the art
together. The writer's the
head of the tale just like the
man's that of the family; the
reader's like the wife in that
she carries the tale into the
world like the wife bears and
delivers a child."

Almost like? Aren't writers
notorious for speaking of their
works as if they were children,
and alive?

who
    is
        a father into
bitter
    sweet
        lament
across
    any
        one
arc
   into
      time, echoing
a loving of God."

   Oft the younger man:
"Come
    fill
      the goblet
of my life with wisdom weave
in pithy phrase up

on a folding through
an end from end to see it
over, whelming all."

"She is so beautiful, when she's full of wrath," Parsafal said.

"Isn't she," Sans said.

"Aye, my friend, aye."

Sans sat down again and continued to watch her.

Parsafal lit a fire and finished cleaning some fish.

The aroma seemed to come before the sound as the meal met the pan, and it was so good.

"I wish she'd taken her things off," Sans said. "She could catch a chill."

"Not enough ground cover, Sans," Parsafal said, wiping his chin.

"Wit! Man and wife only cooperate with the one who does the true creating. Only the reader cooperates, because the writer's the one creating."

You mean that's the crux of what Dante was trying to say in his letter?

"The crux of Dante? I like that. Of course, that's what he meant! The creator of the children doesn't intrude on the mundane talent of the child who's a poet. As if the poem was actually created by he himself! and alive."

We'd be no more than a bitter mote of puppets, if the poet wasn't free. No. The poet's free.

Oft the older man:
"Poured

out for all in

time, too?"

Oft the younger man:

"Have you nothing to

say to me in time?"

"Who me?"

"You, of course."

"Of course."

"Of course. Who else, here?"

"Beyond time."

"Of course."

"Here?

Where nature fled

away to fleer at us in

timeless space beyond

our reach

or ken, too?

Fey wrought upon my brow here

and there where one ought

"What?" Sans asked.

"You would pass through her modesty," Parsafal answered.

"Her modesty?"

"Her modesty."

"I see."

"Exactly."

"She could misunderstand, and think I was trying to invade her intimacy--even undermine her dignity!" Sans said, rubbing his eyes.

"Yes, she could," the knight said as he finished cooking.

"I meant she'd get cold."

"I know. So would she."

She came up to the fire, and smiled.

"Are you sure?"

No.

"No."

No!

"Strange."

Very. I'm beginning to sense that poetry and story are now beyond the grasp of each other in the minds of both the reader and the writer.

"That would make all of this a little pointless, wouldn't it?"

Just a little.

"Only just? It'd be so pointless and meaningless that it'd be both comic and sad. How could story and poetry ever meet?"

none is more than heart

can cry; where numbers bend in

form; to form the time

to try again this

treacherous sea, and sailing

reach the port in time."

They smiled back.

Then, they enjoyed the meal.

Soon, the lovers fell asleep,
holding hands.

Did they ever?

"It's said they one time did."

Or so the story goes from here
to there.

—

DUODECIMUS

Oft the younger man:
"Love singing within
the threads of life: beyond
a raindrop, all rain.

Compassion
                    coming
in the touch of one to one,
all with all; sunrise,

sunsetting,
                    throbbing
intensity
                    seen in love
some chant: man, woman,

orgasmic
                    power,
enhancing
                    some not others
fey
        or not; a bud

blooming

XII

Silence.

Sans snored.

Parsafal smiled as he
looked around the
cupped rim of the
oasis. Over here, from
beyond where he came,
roiling dark and shadow
played out against
fierce strokes of some
primordial light like
lightning--almost. Over
there, from beyond
where they came, a
pulsing glow rippled
back and forth between
the colors--bent. While
within this mere oasis,
it was a calm

Free verse.

"Free prose?"

I don't know. Is what's going on
in poetry going on in prose? If it's
coherent in the one, can it be in the
other?

"How to find out?"

By the doing of it, together.

"Like this."

Yes!

"Coherently?"

Does it have to be perfect?

"Does it matter?"

One ancient tale talks of a land of
utopia. Prosperous and secure, the
citizens of it danced and played.

>   truly seen
> in time of gentle heart,
>   not
> fey in flowers strewn
>
> upon the way
>   in
> seedlings spent; burning lovers'
> lament in eagles?"
>
>   Oft the older man:
> "out and in and out
> to horizons never seen
> in dusk, dawn, dusk, dawn.
>
> Writhing joy
>   some
>   how
> enhancing sorrow to wit
> an end in flowered
>
> thorn.
>   Quest
>   for a truth
> in some

and peaceful place.

"Why is that?" Parsafal asked, himself.

No one answered.

Sans groaned and sat up. "Are you talking to me?" He whispered.

"I was just musing aloud to myself," the knight said.

"About what?"

"About why the calm and peace of our little oasis fails so completely over here as well as over there."

Sans followed the

A visitor came once. He was amazed. Asked to stay.

A certain something bent within their smiles, and a shadow played across their dancing.

He saw this sure, and wondered, why. What was it?

Days later, he finally asked one lone inhabitant about it.

"What is what?" That one asked within a return.

"I don't know. Something. I don't know."

"If you don't know what you're asking, how then can I return to you an answer?"

"I don't know."

"So."

"How do you do it?"

place of veils;

surprise

the dawn at the tip

of

time

on the end

of the earth;

the rising

meets

the setting

in

to

lightning

round

the moon

light;

dusky thrill

without all

around involving

true love

in

arcing

directions of the other's pointing; his eyes widening with each moment, he asked, "It's getting worse, isn't it?"

"Aye," Parsafal said. "What do you think?"

"I'm not sure what to think. I don't see us surviving out in that. Or this."

"Lawk, no, neither do I, Sans."

"We could just stay here."

"The lost memory of who she is and why will soon return,"

"Do what?" The native asked.

"Maintain such peace and plenty," the visitor answered.

"You don't know?"

"Why, no. How could I?"

"I don't know how you can't."

"Well?"

"Well what?"

"How do you do it! I'd like to take your secret home."

"Very well, I'll pretend you really don't know," he said, glancing around them, nervously. Silent, he waited for another man to pass into a building. Then, another. And another. Until there were none around.

The visitor frowned over the other's obvious fear of being

kind, my son, be lust, not love
at all: Thorns in love

speak of truthful mists
that thwart all pride, humbling all
within the scale: dust."

    Oft the younger man:
"Lightning

            come

                  to

                        grounding
strangely twilight to twilight
in words, words, words, words!

Trees
        branching

              to

                  touch
the bird?
          Or

              the

                  alighting
bird branching the tree

in

Parsafal said. "When that happens, the lady will insist on doing what she came to do. You must know it in your heart of hearts, if not within your head."

She said something in her sleep as she turned over.

"What about you?" Sans asked.

"Me?" Parsafal asked in turn.

"What's your doing? What's your task?"

"My task is to search for the Holy Grail."

"Why?"

overheard. He cleared his throat, and wondered if his questions had been wise to ask.

A worker stopped and looked at them, but then passed on by.

The native waited until he was out of sight and hearing, before saying, "It's because those things are seen as being as good as I am. Or so we're taught as children to believe."

"I don't understand," the other said. "What's that got to do with your peace and plenty?"

"We're taught that everyone's as important and precious as everyone else."

"Sounds good."

"Yes, doesn't it."

   the

     root."

  Oft the older man:

       "To see

clearly

   what is,

     is good,

       no?"

  Oft the younger man:

"You

   snare

     me

       with words!"

"A

  clown

    wrapped

      into

sadness

   come on

    the wind

      swept

coasting away in

"I have no recall about it," Parsafal said. "Or of much else about my life before now. Would that I did!"

"What's the first thing you can remember?" He asked.

"Passing this place, just before I met you."

Sans nodded, and looked down at her in thought.

"What about you?" Parsafal asked.

"1 was conceived, and lived my life."

"Like everyone who ever was and is."

"I sense you don't agree," the visitor said.

The native's laugh was much more a sneer as he said, "We're bent into believing that even the most useless and pathetic drudge is worthy of his due."

"So. Tell me more."

"We're taught that that's justice, and that that's why we have this peace and plenty, now."

"I can see some truth in that idea. You can't, I take it?"

"Truth? What kind of truth is it, where that and this and that are seen as being not just as good as I am, but just as important!"

"And you don't agree with the truth of justice?"

naught

      to

         be?"

Oft the younger man:

            "Are you

mocking me?"

Oft the older man:

            "That would be too

easy."

   "Yes or no."

"A little for your
youth seems like a barrier
rain. Listen to me."

"No.

      Why

          should

              I?

               Why?

An old fart lost in the eye
of the heart and mind!

Sans smiled. "I met the don and lived some more, until I met her. And you."

"A simple life," Parsafal said.

"Yes. A simple life."

Some havoc came over the rim as a swirling wind, but then swiftly passed away again to another nothing.

Antigone tossed about, crying in her sleep, but then was still again.

Silence.

Finally, Sans asked, "What's this grail?"

"Agree?" The man's lip curled as he said the word with a shake of his head. "How can I? It'd be a better justice, if I could devour the dregs at any telling need. Justice? To have to treat those things as brothers?"

The visitor said, farewell, and left that place as quickly as he could.

After he had returned home, a friend asked him, "Why rush away like that?"

"I smelled a civil war," he answered. "Or worse."

"Worse?"

"I could almost touch the hatred coming from that man. And, he called it, justice."

"A mystery. I can hardly hold his thought within my soul."

In

    a

        tale

           told

              of

naught

       but strife

           and

              tearing

                  woe

to twist the mind set

of

    an

        age

          a

            part

from

    all

       afore

           in

              timely

flow

    from

"I have never seen it," Parsafal said. "But, I know what it is."

"What is it, then?" Sans probed.

"The Grail is the cup that Christ used at his last supper."

"Can't you find it?"

"Of all the silly things to have to admit. No, I can't. And, I misplaced my horse!"

"Why do you need one of those?"

"Without one of those magnificent beings, a knight is but a fool at court.

'Twas ever thus!

"What was that?"

It was ever thus.

"What was?"

Justice. Justice turning on a lesser need. Or even a mere want. Breaking loose from the foundations of truth where it rightly resides. Power and domination determining what comes under the heading of it.

"Even I can see what happens then."

You can? What happens?

"The widow becomes the prey of the predator. The orphan fodder for war. The poor man becomes a tool."

So it goes. Down through the centuries--.

you

to

me?

Come

now,

tell

me

why?

Tell

me

true!"

Oft the older man:

"Tell

you true in

time to tell of this

and

that?

What

is,

is.

Of what might have been, or what

will be, I know not."

A dangle! Good only
for a toss into some bin
of naught."

"You jest with me,"
Sans said. "You are
who you are. No matter
what."

"Would that that were
so," Parsafal said.
"Would that that were
so, my friend."

"An animal's all you
need to make you what
you hope to be?"

"Exactly."

"That's absurd."

"Absurd?"

"Absurd."

"How so?"

"It's seen as the way of the world.
The way things are. You can't even
define it."

But isn't justice more than a word?

"Define it."

In his quest for man, the God of
Israel says, it's giving the poor their
due at labor and trade. Caring for
the orphan like a son. Loving the
widow
as a sister. Is that definition enough
for you?

"Yes. Enough for me, yes. But to
some it isn't any sort of justice. It's
an unfair restraint on their rights
of power in capacity. So through a
will to use a violent power, justice
is twisted into a parody. A mask. A
form of magical incantation, even."

Oft the younger man:
"You refuse to tell
me?"

Oft the older man:
    "Refuse to tell you that
which fails in any

truth
    in
        time
           or
              place."

"Play the game of wisdom come
amongst us. Aged

thrill
    for
        you
           in
            time
to

"I don't care if
you're sitting on
four or standing
on two," Sans said.
"You're who you are
no matter what the
outcome."

"No matter what?"
Parsafal asked.

"No matter what.
Hold your honor
as you do your
sword. Stand on
the truth as you see
it. Act justly. Love
tenderly. Walk
humbly with your
god."

"Say on."

"Let me think."

"Some would say a
worker, or some

Askew.

"In and out of focus."

Like this aside?

"But with justice gone askew, comes
a war. With this aside, I can only
ask, Is it alive?"

Is it a line, or is it a wave?

"A wave?"

A plot wave.

"That's quite the speculation."

To a point.

"Just."

There's a limit, but where to find it?

"Yes, where?"

I don't know.

"Would thinking help?"

time

    in

        to

           a

                vortex

swelled with what I know

not

    to

        tell

           the

                tale."

Oft the older man:
"What

    do

        I

           tell

              you

                at all

of

    the

        tale?

peasant, is unable to think at all," Parsafal said.

"Who'd say such a thing?" Sans asked.

"Some of the few who see the many as more than less than human."

"Impossible."

"Improbable, but true."

Silence.

"There are really brothers and sisters of mine who think I'm not human, because I'm poor and menial?" Sans asked.

Parsafal nodded.

Maybe, I can think it through, if you'll cease to interrupt me.

"I'll restrain myself."

Very well then, two aspects of reality--.

"Reality? Forgive me. Please, continue."

Two aspects of reality that run counter to our common sense are curious, yet understandable. The first might explain a little why a justice can be twisted into an injustice. The second could explain the meaning of a plot wave.

The one's the oddity that even though most of us grasp and tell the truth of our world as round, our common sense of it still tells us it's flat. But even though we experience it as flat, we

Of

       life?

'Twas

    ever

      thus.

        So

it

  is

    as

      it

       is

        into

life as it is out

side

   to

     side

      the way

is hard and narrow beside

"They do think it true,"
Sans said.

"They do," the knight
said.

"How sad."

"How very sad."

"How could they?"

"You grasp it,
nonetheless."

"Yes."

"Good."

"Good?"

On the other side of
the rim, a tapestry of
lightning spread across
the sky.
Coming from the
direction where the
knight had first

think and feel of it as sphere. We
do this even though our sense in
common tells us it is flat, because
most of us are convinced--and
believe!--the roundness of the world
is true. It took countless years, and
a picture from the moon, for merely
most to see it.

It's the other that's the gathering
point to me in this matter of the
wave. The wave of plot, I mean (to
mean what I say about the beautiful
prism that a written work of art can
be in truth; and love wrought with
all the shadows cast by the light
of life [In delving deeper into the
sensus plenior (A classical grasp of
what the hermeneutic circle can be
is unfolded as an interdependence of
the part and the whole: the

the step by step to

time of dusky scents
too full; off the merely moon
tide swell to changing

chants

      to

            chancing

                  sway

of time; and gravity, well?
all the physical

of

     the

        tale

            of life

pleas
     only

appeared, it ended
somewhere behind
them from where they
had since come.

The ground shook.

A darkness pulsed: a
shadow breathing, in
and out, out and in and
out.

She moaned. Sat up and
glanced around. Smiled
at Sans. Placed her head
on his lap, and went
back to sleep.

He stroked her brow
and smiled longingly
at her for some time.
Then, he looked up
at Parsafal, and his
smile faded away into a
sudden fear.

whole can be understood only
through its parts, but the parts can
be understood only through the
whole. Beyond the one's the other
sounding backwards and forwards
upon each and every part as they
each and every one reflects the
whole in telling all the parts. Or,
the one's seen in the many, and the
many in the one. Be [it as it may be
throughout the tale, the
story folds and unfolds as a story
pure and not so simple:

In another time, there was some
comic relief.

A joke was just a joke.

A sigh was just a sigh (toward a time
along the way to know).

Was it just? This joke of jokes. Was
it? Some had said civilization hung
in the balance.

the

        merest

           part

of all wholeness seen
through

    out

      glimpses

          felt

be

  yond

    the

      tide

        in

          time

            less

trek

  to

The knight's face was drained of color, and his finger raised to point toward the rim.

Sans' eyes followed it and stopped at the figure on that rim.

If he it was, the figure, being wreathed in shadows within shadows, echoed the sky around. A knight in black sitting on a great steed of black. This man's eyes glowed with a fathomless and pulsing red; while, flames came from the nostrils of the

Relief was a necessity, after all. So what if so many were to die to laugh in such a way?

Great care was taken to protect the sons and daughters of all culture against that deadly thing. Triple linguistic drifts across the core of its meaning and double translation fields were used for this, but even so, some of them were lost to the cause.

The key that had led to the breakthrough was the understanding that laughter can be sometimes infective, spreading swiftly through a crowd. Uncontrollable, it often took the breath away. Taking the breath away, it affected the heart. With some refinement in delivery and technique, the joke was made, and given out to use with such

drop

     by

       drop

of

  rain

     to

       rain in

between

   the

    lightning

      branching

destiny, flying

over

  mountain

horse.

"What is that?" Sans whispered.

"Nemesis," Parsafal answered. "My nemesis."

"Good Lord. You have to face that?"

"Aye. Him."

"And you've been waiting here for him?"

"Aye."

The figure turned in its shadows, and disappeared beyond the rim.

"I could've sworn that rim just moved closer," Sans said,

a devastating effect, it was to bring a tear to tear the heart.

Great care was taken with the very few unprotected copies of it:

"Warning:

'If you have any sense of humor, do not, under any circumstances, open.'

'For humorless eyes only!'

'Stop! only the dour beyond this point!'"

The joke was used.

With effect.

Far and wide, until the war was won.

Won?

(There once was an old priest

gold

still falling drop by drop by

drop with light between."

   Oft the younger man:

"What am I to make

of this twaddle within this

play of flying birds

that

    you

        call

            word

              song?

Your age does show your plight in

time to be so young

no

   more;

       and

and that rim did actually move closer to them then.

"Aye," Parsafal said. "I think you speak the truth."

"Is that why you need a horse?"

"Would a steed for me be too much to ask?"

"We can only act on what we have. But, who is that? your nemesis."

"He is that one who stands between me and that for which I search. Between me and that most holy prize, he stands!"

who took his golf game very seriously. So seriously that even over the protests of his bishop, he had taken his old biretta out of storage to wear for luck upon the course.

He played.

And played.

Each time his wrath would rise anew at each imperfection in his game.

Venting with a roar, he'd cast down his club, and looking up to heaven, cry out, "A true game to play be all I'm asking!"

As time passed, the other players-- beginning with the bishop--passed him by. They mocked him behind his back. They mocked him-- especially, when he talked to God, not them.

envy

strips

you

bare

to

hueless

bone

within the eyelids

of

a

time

some

call

history

with

out

a

tale

of

woe

"Don't you mean sit?" Sans asked.

Parsafal just looked at him.

"Are you going on with it?"

"How can I?"

"I still say, you don't need a horse."

"You saw him. How can you say that, now?"

"I saw him. I say it still."

"Are you mad?"

"Wouldn't face that one, even with a herd."

"Not even for love?"

So soon only God and his angels were seeing his game, and that on only the shortest of all courses.

Early one morning at the start of a very lonely round, he said to the sky, "Ar, surely your angels're mocking me, Lord."

He groaned as he set the ball on the tee.

"You and m'self, Lord," he said as he addressed it, and made one beautiful swing.

That ball arced to the green, landing just inside the edge; rolled on up to the cup, dropping in as sweet as you please.

"You wouldn't be mocking this old sinner, would you, Lord?"

    and

        twain

           be

side

  a

    stillness

          spent.
Falling

    down

        in

          to

            the

              night,

shading out inside

a

    shadow

        playing

on the mind without a hope

The ground shook.

The oasis shrank a little more.

The sky writhed.

"How important's this quest to you?" Sans asked.

"Aye, you pass the rub to me, dear man," Parsafal said. "At the heart of it is the why of what I do."

"And?" Sans asked as he watched a somewhat darker shadow creep over the rim, and then crawl back. "How important is this grail to you?"

No one else was around.

He went to the second tee, and the same thing happened.

Onto the third, and once again.

The fourth, fifth, sixth--the whole of the front nine; and onto the back ones, the same--the tenth, eleventh and twelfth.

The old man looked around at the fifteenth tee, and saw no one else around.

"How is it you'd be giving me this now?" He asked as he concentrated on the ball. "When tomorrow after today with none to see it, I'll still be knowing there's no future in the past. Only now beyond the future of the past."

of something more or

less in time to be
in thought or deed at need or
needless heed the quest!"

    Oft the older man: Sighed.

    Oft the younger man:
"What?"
       "You
            seek
                a
                   quest?"
"Live and fly into a dark
dust and desert rain?"

"So
    in
        you
            the
               drab
lament
       in
           quest

"Very," Parsafal
answered.

"Why?" Sans asked.

"'Tis but a sign
within itself. A sign
of selfless love. A
sign of the one who
held it once. I quest
for it, because I
quest for him."

"You don't need a
horse."

"Say on."

"I say, this shadow
within a shadow,
you'll have to face.
As to that honor
and nobility you set
so high a sway on?
What does a drudge
know of

Silence.

He swung his club.

The ball arced high.

And down into the cup.

Silence.

So again, at the sixteenth.

On the seventeenth, once again.

At the eighteenth tee, he looked
up to heaven with a sudden smile
grown gentle, peaceful, calm.

He shrugged.

Made a sign of the cross on himself,
and swung.

And into the cup.

Later, he was sitting at the
nineteenth hole, and his bishop
walked in before the

       foreseen

          by

all in wholesome dread

has

    come

       so

         soon

           to

see

    the light

       in

         shadows

           dark

as

  some

    would

      see

        in

night

  and

    shade

      be

        yond

such things? But
didn't the one whose
sign you seek ride in
triumph on an ass?
It seems to me that
a walking to a sign
of such a one holds
in it no dishonor,
nor ignobility. Fear.
Your fear's very
understandable. But
fear it only is that has
you calling for
a horse."

The ground shook.

"Drudge?" The good
knight said with a
wan smile. "Worker?
Peasant? Aye. Would
that all would be so,
if all be such as you,
my brother. Would all
were so!"

start of his own game. The old man
began to rise, but the other one told
him to stay.

"Another bad round, Shawn?" The
bishop asked, ordering a drink but
not sitting.

"Why, no, m'lord," he answered.

"No," the apostle said in dawning
wonder at the manner of the man.

"No, m'lord," old Shawn said. "The
perfect round."

"Sure, and you've gobbled now the
stone entire!"

"And the joke's on me.")

The war is won!

But not the gift of any peace.

a star

      inside

           or

               out

                    side

of time on finding

out

      the

           quest

               in

                    side

us; somehow on the outside

in the question, true

dark comes down seeking

light as a complementing

trace of dusk in quest."

   Oft the younger man:

"Aye,

      a quest

           I

               seek

away from noting sway on

"Honored," Sans
whispered, looking
down to hide a tear.

A number of balls of
lightning swept up
from where the dark
knight had shown
himself, passed over
the oasis, and fell onto
the other rim side over
there.

"That grabbed your
attention!" They both
said at the same time.

They laughed.

And cried.

And laughed.

Sitting up and
yawning, Antigone
said, "Fill me too

Some said laughter died that
day, and only the dour remained.
Others that it only rested for a
clown to come again] aware of
it, and laugh) and finding there
a deeper, more biblical, meaning
in the word repentance: Going
beyond the boundaries of our
minds and times into a mystery
so simple and so sublime, it could
embrace even the greatest one of
all, if that one had the humble
wisdom to hug it back.

Love back.

Here as I dimly see a finger of
my god, I also see only so far
and only so deeply into this idea
of the sensus plenior; and claim
here a silence now as a much
better course for me] beyond that
life or this one) time: The other
gathering point to me in this
matter of the

you and kith or kin."

    Oft the older man:
"In

        other

            words,

                you

would seek

          for her

              over

                    there

across the wayfare

of

    it

        and

            of time

bemused

        in

            struggles

                ancient

wrought

        by mind

            to

with your levity!"

Having stifled most
of it as she spoke, the
laughter burst out of
them, again.

"What?" She asked,
looking down at
herself and then back
up at them.

They stopped, and
after gazing at her for a
time, laughed, again.

"Are you mocking me
to my face?" Antigone
asked, standing up
and then sitting down
again with the merest
touch of grace. "How
could either of you be
doing so to me?"

plotting wave.

"Time?"

Time.

"Time. Enough to make these
thoughts thinkable? if not altogether
readable."

Time enough.

"Enough! Tell me what you're
thinking, fool."

About a hundred years ago,
a not so simple man showed
us, mathematically, that time's
intimately bound up in the tendrils
of the spatial. Even though our
common senses tell us otherwise,
both are very fluid, mixing in and
affecting each other in the most
utterly intriguing ways. Space
warping time; time bending and
then straightening space all at once.

core
of
heart
up
on some
sweep
of
time
that swirls in tides
of what still might have
been
to
stay
in true
vastness fast to stay entwined;
indulging so as

not to merge but thrive
in the warp and woof of shock
and struggle in life."

Oft the younger man:
"Aye,

"No!" Sans said,
wiping away a tear.

"Certainly not!"
Parsafal said.

The ground shook.

The shadows rose and
fell.

Lightning pulsed in
and out of being.

Then, the mounted
knight rode into sight
at the lip of the rim.
Blood red was the
pennant on his lance
with but a stroke of
black upon it. Dipping
it toward the goodly
one, he reared his steed
up on the hind

"Christ on ice! You do go on, don't
you?"

And why not7

"Who understands enough about
it to make any sense out of what
you're saying? I don't, and I'm right
here with you. Can anyone really
understand those equations, or your
thoughts about them?"

I don't know. Some.

"Some? Just some?"

Enough for some to be testing
those equated thoughts. Some
of those are showing the four
dimensions as being but one whole
continuum with an edge. Even
more, other dimensions are seen in
those thoughts beyond our sensory
capacity to see or hear or feel or
smell or taste--beyond our ken to

a quest

I seek!

She, alone! not craven as some

who under the veil

of duty

stay

in

a shroud

of wary

warmth,

cutting off courage

fore

ever

into

the heart

of a man

in time,

duty

and

honor."

"Bound

the bond

legs wreathed in flame
and shadow. Down
again, he turned and
went back away beyond
their sight, leaving
only the starkness of
the challenge.

"What was that?" She
asked.

"A man and his horse,"
Sans said.

"A man and his horse?"

"A mere man, and
his horse," Parsafal
answered with a wry
smile.

Silence.

Sans cleared his throat,
and asked the

imagine. Like the squared circle,
it--.

"What?"

It can be thought, but not imagined
into existence.

"Are you saying, the nth dimension
can be thought, yet not imagined?"

Yes.

"But the oneness of time and space
can be."

And is. It's beginning to be seen,
and heard. Felt enough to grow a
wave of plotting.

"I don't know. It's just a secondary
world we're into now."

But in this secondary world of
literary angst, the upheavals within
the spatial dimensions,

       of heart
and home
      ward step
          and striding
love filled gut and grind
that
    groans
       blooded field

on field on field on field in
some bone of epic

timing grasp and reach
of novel trial and struggle
of mind and heart."

"Aye,
     quest in honor
calls me to follow her."
"Aye. So be it so.

Passion fails.
     So do
you more so,
      and seek your grail!
Remember your name,

knight, "You're going
out to meet him, aren't
you?"

"Aye, I go to meet him,"
Parsafal said, checking
his gear and testing the
sweep of his sword.

"Without a horse."

"Aye."

Sans came to him,
just avoiding the last
sweep of the sword, and
embraced him, heartily.

Parsafal walked over to
where she still sat, and
gently took her hand to
kiss it once, or twice, or
thrice.

holding true within it, are reflected
in the one called time.

"Are you saying, when that questing
knight passed over from the realm
of poetry into the land of prose,
time as well as space folded--and
bending!--unfolded him into the
past of this land, over here?"

Simple.

"Simple, he says--and he's penciled
me into sounding like him, too!"

Don't you see, space and time
are one. If the one's in a chaotic
disharmony, so's the other. Just
because the gut doesn't feel it,
doesn't make it any less the truth.

"Are you trying to say the

Parsafal.

      Go. Find

her,

    but more the cup in all

honor,

      bending low."

"Farewell,

      good mentor."

"Go.

      I shall hold it here; there,

too--alone, as may

be so,

      no matter

the chaos be so coming

in and out to be

so now and then; fare

well within your quest, my child,

until met again."

She stood into Sans'
arms, and holding one
another, they watched
the knight turn firmly
to the rim.

The ground shook.

Parsafal stood silent for
a moment; then strode
with a gathering vigor
to it, was over and gone
away from them.

The rim moved closer
still.

  (Chaos.
Order.

  Chaos.
Order.
  Chaos.)

primary world's bound that tightly
together?"

I don't know. Maybe. It would
allow a place for compassion.
Maybe I'm just saying, the arts of
reading and writing are one.

"A formalist would see it one
way; a deconstructionist, another.
Wouldn't they?"

Even the most radical would
have to allow the realm and the
land are one over here and there.
Touch this word here, and it
affects that stanza there; touch
that metaphor there, and it affects
this sentence here into a tale of
once or twice upon a time.

—

TERTIUS DECIMUS

(Chaos.

Order.

Chaos.

Order.)

"Along an inner

calm alone to wind a tree;

bending in the root,

a soil

tells the tale

before the budding bond in

quest of fruit to feed

a one,

or more--some

play--,

and cast the seed upon

a soil; once for all

impressions

left through

generations

XIII

(Chaos.

Order.

Chaos.

Order.)

The rim squeezed
closer as they stood
almost waiting
for him to come
back over the lip.
But, they rather
waited with a dread
between them. A
dread that almost
stayed between
them, but failed to
do so once again.
But still, the dread
told them for whom
they stood, and
waited.

They trembled,
and held each
other closer.

The wind hit
him hard enough
to knock him
down, but he
stood his ground
without a motion
for the moment.
Then, leaning
fully forward, he
pressed on toward
his destiny.

(Chaos. Order.
Chaos. Order!
Chaos! Order.
Chaos. Order!)

To think or not to
think isn't even a
viable question.

"It's a thought."

Or not.

"If it weren't such
a craven pose to
be thoughtless,
it'd be easier."

And much safer.

"It would be that.
Thoughtlessness.
A void avoiding."

       rooted in
to seasons
       yawning

time
     in centuries
of a soil
       within a soil;
so one angel chants

an echo
       of the whole
eternity as a seed
within a woman

pure in eye without
a veil between her sorrow
and her joy; rooted

passed
     a plighting
          flow;
ebb: Moonscape etching shadows
toward a mountain,

becoming

Then, let go, and looked, one to the other.

"You expect his nemesis to come over the rim," she said, rather than asked.

"It's what I'd do, if I were him," Sans said. "Sounder principle to deal with the lesser, first."

"What can we do?"

"I don't know."

"But you know what that shadow will do."

"Maybe. What do you think?"

Parsafal tried to keep an eye open, but it was impossible. He could barely breathe as the ground he was walking on began to fill the air. Even then, the glow of the lightning sometimes passed through his aching eyelids.

He fell.

Got up.

Fell down.

And got up.

The storm began to ease, but the

And you call me the fool.

"Thoughtlessness as an act of will has caused much more than mischief in our history. Has it not?"

(Chaos.

Order.

Chaos.

Order.)

It would be much better to will to love and think.

"Wouldn't it."

Maybe.

"If you chose

          sand

              on

the shore

        of some sea

              eons

from when? time edging.

Lost amongst

         the

            trees

and never

       to be

         but felled

with woe

       to

        a soul

in a veil

      of

        time

on a song

        sighing

           twice sought

longing; spiraling

here and there

"I am confounded,"
Antigone answered.

"So am I, my love,"
Sans said. "I could
quick make a staff."
Taking out his long
knife, he idly played
with it. "For all the
good it'll do us."

"Quick make me
one, too!"

"You?"

"Aye! Do I appear
crippled to you?"

"No."

"Well?"

So, he quickly
carved her one, and
then, himself.

lightning balls
and strokes were
intensifying.

He halted.

Slowly, he eased
open his eyes.
Then, he dropped
his jaw, aghast.
But spat and
gagged out the
sand that came
in for his trouble.
He bent over into
what was left of
the winds, and
heaved out his
insides. Then,
he stood, and
roughly rubbed
his face.

"Better," he

not to think,
would love
have a human
meaning?"

If I'm truly who
I'm meant to be,
no.

"Interesting."

It's so clear to
me the lack of
thought on the
part of another
person does
not diminish
her humanity. I
know I need to
be transparent
for you on this.
Without it, you'd
misunderstand
me. Nothing
can break our
common bond.
To me.

                        in

                           to

paradox so orthodox

in ground of being

true and sound in one

and three in one through moonlight

in a rising sun; light

through

            some

                  rolling

                        mist

fall dawn the seed of dusk so

set the noon in drop

through

            drop

                out

                    drop by

time

        in drop

              by drop

                    in pale

reflected mistral

She thanked him as he handed her one.

He nodded.

They crossed their staves. Almost formal, it seemed a testing, one of the other for a moment- with a pass or two or three, maybe.

Sans wrapped his hands together on his staff, planting it on the ground beside his feet. Leaning his cheek against it, he smiled, saying, "You're no cripple, my lady. That's for sure."

"No more than that, you dare to say?"

said, looking around.

The shadows on the landscape mirrored the light and dark roiling of the sky. The wind settled away. Not one bolt or ball flew across the way.

Silence.

"Where are you in all of this?" Parsafal asked of that scape, both land and sky. "Where in all of this?"

A horn winded from out of some

"To you."

Yes, to me.

"Better you, than me."

If someone chose not to think, he could choose to love at the same time. But because the love was so thoughtless, wouldn't it be somewhat twisted through that choice to be less than the best? Not the lack of it so much as the choice to be in lack of it.

"What a strange way to see it."

rain

    of

        fulsome

            knot

with

    in

        fore

           gotten

              place or

maze

    be

        musing

           some,

not

    all;

        to be,

           but

never

    not

        to be;

           fore ward

a word as word, too.

In

He held up his hand
as she returned to
a fighting stance,
and said, "Hold,
woman! Save your
mastery for a better
foe."

"I doubt there is
such a one, Sir
Drudge," she said.

"You heard me as I
babbled, did you?"

She laughed.

"Are you mocking
me?" He asked,
almost laughing,
too.

"No, my Sans! But
for your babbling,
Parsafal would not
have seen you true
as brother to him.
So, no, my love,
I would

where in the
distance ahead
of him, unseen.

Reaching back
into a fold of
his cloak, he
brought out a
small skin of
water, and took
a swallow. Put
it back and
pulled out a
small ram's
horn. He blew
it, once. Then,
again. Only to
sling it over his
shoulder and
close his eyes
to listen with
his heart as
he waited for
an answer.

(Chaos.

Order.

Chaos.

Order.)

Did you feel that?

"In a sense."

In a sense?

"Yes, in a sense. I
sense the folding
and unfolding
of a story, or a
poem. This or
that."

So, you
understand!

"Are you asking
if I stand beneath
the arc of this?
Under the weave
of that or this?"

       to

           an

               echo

of a plight on troth under

the musk of bridal

ecstasy in time

and space; born with all some awe

in shades of moon

and

     star

         in

            mist

               sphere

come; or a pale covenant

throughout and beside

a

   sky;

      just

         to

           see

what

   is,

never mock you."
Then, she reached
over, and caressed
his cheek.

"I do go on like a
wind," Sans said.

Silence.

They turned toward
the rim, and waited.

Awaited.

And waited.

Finally, she said,
"This fails us. How
can we do nothing?"

"Another sound
path is to take
down the stronger
foe, first," Sans
whispered, gripping
his staff so tightly

In a moment,
the other horn
sounded once
from far away.

"So, why not
come for me,
now? Not for
those I left
behind! Over
there. Foul shade
of man! To me,
you will come!"

He grabbed his
horn, and blew it,
again.

Then, silence.

"Nothing," he
whispered.

But, a moment
later, the other

I don't
understand.

"I know. But, you
hope I do."

Hope? Hope. I
feel like a hole,
where a person
ought to be.
Hope. What
hope?

"So a hole you
are. A poet. A
writer. A teller
of tales. A hole
through which
such an havoc
can be wrought
as to seize the
tongue, and time.
Maybe, your hole
just isn't large
enough to meet
the challenge

                        is

                            no

                                more nor no

less a destiny

be

        yond

                that

                        full

                                fate

of

        man

                and

                        woman

                                one or

not,

        in

                time

                        to

                                be

still

        less

                than

                        all

that a cracking
sound was heard.

"So, he might not
be coming for us,"
she said.

"Maybe," he said.

"What do you
suggest?"

"Eat."

"Eat?"

"Eat, and drink.
Notice the skins
of water and fish
by the fire? He left
them for us."

"What do you
propose? We eat,
drink, and be
merry. So merry we
forget our friend?"

one sounded
closer still.

Again, a silence.

On a rise, just
before him, the
dark knight
rode into view.
He dismounted.
Said something
to his steed.
Then, alone, he
walked slowly
toward him.

Parsafal girded
himself.

A few paces away,
the other knight
stopped.

They glared at
each other.

of the word."

Are you
challenging me to
the duel?

"The duel of wit
and word, you
mean?"

Yes, that duel.

"Fool!"

Now that's a
choice bit of
drollery. You'd
best keep such
a turn of phrase
for our coming
contest, and not
waste it on this
sparring.

"Contest? Hardly
that."

Do you
withdraw?

on

an

ebb

and

a

flow of words.
Listen to silence?

Sound

the

horn

of

naught?

Not to place a knot within
some tongue into cheek.

Or, a clear hammer
striking nails, and caldera
of the galaxies.

Or,

a

lark

"And tomorrow, die?" Sans asked. "Maybe. But, no. To follow."

"I knew I fell in love with you for some goodly reason," she said, kissing him. "When do we go?"

"Now. Let's gather what we can, and eat and drink on the way. No time. This calm may pass away."

They quickly gathered what they could, and strode up to the rim. But pausing for a moment, they pulled in their courage with a deep breath, and then went

"What would you of me, sir?" Parsafal asked.

"Satisfaction," the other's voice sounded hollow through his visor as he spoke; but, his eyes glowed red through the eyelets.

"You demand a satisfaction from me?"

"Indeed."

"How, in deed, have I given you offense?"

"Fool, and no knight in being

"Withdraw? Hardly, before such as you."

Then, a duel drawn with word and wit between us, I accept.

"I knew that. What form do you follow?"

Form? I don't understand.

"No? Never done one?"

No. Never.

"Sweet."

Not bitter? Or maybe, both? What weave of form are you playing me

                singing
blue whispers in a remnant
played for downbursting

time

        to

            catch

                the

                    sky.

Or,
      drop

          by

              plodding

                  drop

                     in

time to time to try

in

      step

          by

              step

                  to

be

down into the
broken landscape.

Silence.

They marched.

And listened.

Listened for the
ram's horn.

And marched.

They ate and drank
as they walked in
silence.

And listened.

Hoped they moved
toward the knight.

But still listened for
that horn.

Silence played along
the edge of all that
could be seen.

so," the dark
one said with a
sardonic laugh
that fled slowly
into the firming
silence.

"Answer my
question, sir,"
Parsafal said.

"Very well, sir
pirate. In passing
by here earlier,
you raided my
supply depot.
Then to add
insult to injury,
you and your
people are
squatting in my
oasis. Does that
answer your
question, sir
pirate foul?"

into now?

"None untoward,
if you can believe
it. I yearn for the
crossing of
a word for word
with you. Fair,
not foul."

Then, I take you
at your word.

"Good."

What would you
suggest?

"That would
depend on you."

On me? Why on
me?

"You're the
challenged."

So?

in

hope

through

echoes

on

an

edge

on

time.

Or,

sweep

of

silence

in

the

one

soul

one

has

to play

The arc of the sky
turned as if it were
a personal threat
to them. Darkness
shattered the light.
Falling on the land,
the remnant of
that light was met
by another kind of
shadow, and failed,
completely. Tendrils
of mist rose out of
the ground, and
gathered far above
their heads.

"How can we find
our way in this?"
She whispered.

In the distance, a
large piece of land
exploded in flames.

The ground shook.

In the ensuing
silence around
them, Parsafal
looked down.

"Does that
answer your
question?" The
other one asked.

"Indeed, sir," the
goodly one said,
looking up. "My
most humble
apologies. All
I can offer in
my stead is my
ignorance of your
claim."

"That is of no
satisfaction to
me."

"The northern
rules call for you
to choose the
form, and offer
first what it is you
have to give. In
the southern, I
choose the form,
and you go first.
In the eastern,
you choose the
form. I go first.
The western turns
the other way
around. I have no
preference. So,
choose. You're
mine to end in
any case."

End? To what
end are you
meaning to imply
by end?

and seek a time in

to
   life
      be

         yond
           some

envelope within the eye
of one mind and heart.

Placing the oar with
the water, the surface parts
to see the folding

depths

     of
       tide
         in
           tide

to time the falling shadow
of some passing phase

up

"I don't know," Sans finally answered. "Try. We can only try."

"Aye," she said. "Try."

On they went, but soon their steps were stumbling ones.

Then, just as their hearts were starting to fail them, they looked up at a rise in the distance, and saw an object standing against the sky. It grew darker as they neared. The edge of it grew sharper with its size and bulk against that roiling sky.

"What do you propose?" Parsafal asked.

"What I propose is to give you one of three alternatives to choose," the dark knight said with an arrogant air.

"And these are what?"

"The first is for you to fall upon your steel--if you have any honor."

"The second?"

"The second is for you and your people to serve

"Just that. The end of the one who fails in the contest."

You're joking.

"Not at all."

And how can one of us end, who hasn't a beginning?

"By never again chanting a poem, or telling a tale."

I understand.

"Good. And your choices?"

Prose the form.

"And who first?"

It'd be the best for me to be the

on

the

surface

of

a

lunar

scape

and

gaze

upon an earthen

sky

in

hues

be

yond

a

heart

"Horse," Sans said in a whisper, and motioned for her to get down with him behind a dune.

Close against him, Antigone whispered, "If the wind comes, that one will smell us for sure."

"But for now, he doesn't know we're here. He's fixed on what's happening down there."

"What can we do?"

He pointed along a long ribbon of sand leading from the tiny dune to a little cut on the rim of the hill near the horse.

me."

"And the last?" Parsafal asked.

"Last?" The dark one echoed.

"Aye, the last."

To fall on my steel, and so regain what was once called your honor."

Silence.

With an ugly laugh, the dark knight added, "You have until the coming of the wind to decide your course. I await

first.

"Good. All the better for me to dispel you."

Any more rules I need to know?

"No. None."

Once (many moons from now), there was a land where never tale was told--.

"Nor poem sung?"

Nor poem sung.

"I thought as much!"

Because that duty to the common good had been pushed outside the bond or

        mind

           to

             grasp

                in

time

    of

       woe

         or

           joy

or

   both

      in

        echoes

of

  a

    tide

      be

"We'll crawl to
that--without a
sound."

She nodded.

"Good," he said in
an even lower kind
of whisper. "So
far. I think they're
talking over there;
and if we can chase
away his horse,
he might have a
chance against that
monster."

"Done," she said,
starting to crawl
away from him.

"Wait," he said,
pulling her back.

"What?"

"we have to be very
careful in how we
approach that beast.

your choice with
an eagerness I
find difficult to
express in words."

Parsafal gazed
beyond the other
at the sky.

Silence.

The dark one
laughed and
shook his head.

The sky beyond
him, where
the goodly one
was looking,
glowed and
pulsed around
a small white
light- almost too
intense to hold a
sense.

of law, the poem
and the story
were all but gone.

"You're kidding
me. You are a
fool. A clown!"

Yes! A clown had
been the first and
last to push the
powers into such
a drastic move.
The art of the tale
had grown into a
pale and hollow
mist. Only good
for wealth, and
maybe, power.

"And prestige,
maybe?"

Maybe so. All
would hear, but

yond

both

spheres.

Or, false paradox?

A

shade

still

into

a shadow round a light in
time to grasp upon

the eye of the heart;
branching earth to star dusting
ebb, and flow one on

through

two

or

three

or

If we attack it directly, it will simply kill us."

"What do you propose?" She asked.

"That we scare the thing," he answered. "Up there, we rise as one out of nowhere. You on my shoulders, and both of us swinging our staves--and without a sound."

Together and silently, they crawled as quickly as they could to the rim; and saw the dark one turn away. Then, she was upon his shoulders.

The horse only

"The wind will come," the other said, and very slowly turned to retrace his steps.

The white light grew, and the penumbra around it spread out through other colors.

Somehow.

Parsafal threw down his sword, and the hilt stuck deeply in the sand.

The dark knight looked up, and saw the strange figure costing

none, except for maybe a few, listened, anymore.

"Can you blame them?"

That first clown wondered long on your very question. Long, he wondered. Long, he pondered the meaning of his acting, and the laughter of it all.

"How long was that?"

Not long.

"That's good, you fool."

And a comic relief as well.

more to tell the tale in awe
of beauty inward
and

    out

        ward

            in

                play

to

   sing

      the

        song

           of

              life be

yond all ken? so, life

flows

     and

        ebbs

          be

            yond

all

   ken

noticed them as
they sped toward
him; and fled away
in terror.

She climbed down.

He steadied her;
and they both
turned at the
cry coming from
behind them.

"Steady, my love,"
Sans said, stepping
away. "You strike
high, and I, low."

"I love you," she had
been saying as the
sound of the horn
reached them.

They drew together,
and watched with
a sinking feeling of
helplessness as the
duel below rushed

him, dearly. He
roared in rage,
and started
striding toward
the remaining
figure--now two!

Parsafal took out
his horn, and
placed it to his
lips and blew.

His nemesis
halted his march
and turned to
him, slowly.
Then, he strode
back, drawing out
his blade.

Pointing his
finger to the
light, Parsafal
knelt with a

"Spare me."

Another rule
I should know
about?

"No. No other.
None!"

Good. I did
wonder, if one
or two I hadn't
heard from you.

"No, none."

Again, good!
Shall I go on with
it? Good. I think
I will:

"What can
I do?" That
clown asked,
himself.

A silence

in

this

flower

or

that

shell

curving

in

to

here

and

there

to

be

of

passing

in

and

out

of sense and focus;

toward an end.

They turned toward
where he seemed
to be pointing, and
gasped. All words
within them failed
to grasp and tell
of who they saw.
While a trembling
awe was all that
kept their sight
intact.

Then, with the
sound of the battle
cry, they looked
back down at the
spectacle.

Behind them, the
light folded away
into the shadows.

Darkness gathered,
and then spread out
farther.

The wind rose,

look of wonder,
ignoring the
onrushing man.

And he ran him
through with a
roar of rage and
glee; and while
struggling to pull
out the blade,
he fell backward
onto the upturned
sword, twitching
for a time.

Soon the bodies
were still--like
brothers; but
Parsafal's own
groaned, alone.

And as the sand
rose into the
wind, he dreamt:

answered.

"Thought as
much," he said to
the sky. "You'd
think I'd, at least,
have something
to offer." Then, he
looked down into
his pail, and saw
but a coin or two
for his trouble
and the laughter.
"Once a fool."
He scratched
his head with
a groan. "Now
what?" He
sighed. "Think!"
He sat down, and

so

    as

       to

         tell

           in

timing tale, an all within

a naught but a mage

in word and symbol,

sign and wonder? work and play

in a morion

prism;

      sing

        in

          some

song shaping tides of timing,

and of an echo,

in

    to

       kith

          in

swiftly.

Lightning, both ball
and bolt, etched out
and in of the roiling
land and skyscapes.

Stronger still grew
the coming of the
winds in time.

As they watched
the sandstorm
cover the distant
forms, she buried
herself against him,
weeping. Together,
they turned and
staggered down and
away.

With an ever
growing intensity,
the winds and their
sisters were beating
upon them with
what seemed a
ruthlessness beyond

Of a flower.

"A rose," he
whispered.

And so it was a
red rose.

Long, he sat,
watching it
unfold, and then
fold away again.
He awakened
into a very intense
awareness of the
interdependence,
the harmony! of
all that is, and
was, and ever will
be.

Harmony.

Then, it died.

He wondered if
he cowered,

tried to do just
that for a little
while.

But soon again, a
few people were
gathering around
him, asking for a
story.

Nodding, he
closed his eyes,
and told them
one. Without
looking, he heard
them laughing as
he finished with
it. When that
sound was surely
fading away, he
opened his eyes,
and glanced into

       kind.

Along

    an edge

      of

       some

        eye

in a storm without

a

  mote

    through

      ice

       bound

seas

  between

    a rage

      to

       see

a

  hue,

    two

     or

      three.

Wry

despair.

Sans forced his way
onward to what he
hoped would be the
oasis.

And, she followed
him.

Forever seemed the
time in passing.

Strange!

In passing.

Until, they stumbled
over the lip of the
rim, and rolled down
almost to the edge of
the water.

The wind eased into
a silence.

Except for the voice
of her mourning.

falling (into a
deeper dream:

He sat in a home.

A mother held
an infant in a
rocking chair.
Before a roaring
fireplace, she
sang, but he
failed to hear the
lyrics through the
rhythm of that
fire. Yet, he could
hear the crack
of the chair as it
moved.

Back and forth.

Outside, the wind
rose with a

the pail to see
what they

had given for the
jest.

It was empty.

"So heartless
wonders!" He
cried. "Was the
tale so foul? Was
your laughter so
distasteful to you?
My pail's for your
hearts to give.
Tradition says so!
Was it truly the
tale that was so
foul, or your lack
of heart? Why
take from me my
little

    jest

        in

           time,

              less

the more

    to hear

        a

           woe,

              where

is the sting or mark?

To

    leave

        naught

           a

              mark

nor sway upon the prism
of time, and only

an if of a tale?
Truth to tell of a lie or
flower--of passion

in

    and

He tried to comfort her.

She said, something.

"What?"

"I remember."

"What do you remember?"

"Parsafal."

"He was one of great honor," Sans said, stroking her hair. Then, taking out his water skin, he put it in her hands.

She emptied it.

"Better?"

"Aye. Thank you, beloved."

He nodded, sighing.

roar.

And fell away.

With only then the sounds of rocking and the fire around, he watched a single tear, running crimson down the mother's cheek. His sensing of the scarlet tear expanded with a pulsing sympathy to those sounds. Then, it gathered the focus of his mind, folding over [and collapsing his world into some other one so much deeper now

bit of coin? My coin to eat this day."

"You know all coin and power are for the great and few!" A voice said from behind him.

The clown stood up quickly, turning around and leaving his pail between them.

The other man glanced down at it, fingering the badge on his vest.

"The tradition

       out

           of time.
The shading of the yearning
bud foreshadowing

shards

       of

            darkness

                   come

to

     passing

          over

              lightning?
Still shards of darkness

held

     within

          the

            palm.
Tales

     entwined

          in telling

              muse

be

   yond

"I remember," she
whispered.

"What else can you
remember?" He
asked.

"Who I am."

"Yes?"

"And, who he was."

"Who was he?"

"My betrothed."

Sans was silent, but
his gentle touch and
gesture said enough
of his love for her.

Antigone wiped her
tears, and smiled.

He kissed her.

The ground shook.

It waned, but she

within him:

In a silence, he
was himself,
again. One who
remembered he
had been young
once.

Very young,
he gazed at
a sanctuary,
glowing golden
with an argent
hue of shadow.

Abandoned.

Angelic waves,
horizons long,
sang in love; and
although he failed
to hear, he felt it.

Shattered.

allows me my
open pail for any
coin or folding,
sir," The clown
said with a
growing outrage
at this man and
his temerity.
Never had a
minion of the
powers dared to
stoop to so brazen
a gesture of
injustice. "Would
you take away my
bread? My art?
My life?"

"That tradition
now is void in
law," the

      all

         mortal

ken;

     dirt

        and

           dusting

tale

    in telling

        chime

          chant

the twin of daylight.

Dusk   {Chaos.

    to

      dawn

        by   Order.

orb orisons long aside   Chaos.

a glass of waters

still in time; beyond

a sky beneath all ken to

see a jest, defined.   Order.)

Crystal

    miming--."

bent onto his hand
and held it to her
lips. Then, she took
a deep breath and
stood up, saying, "I
must go back over
there."

Breathing deeply, he
too stood, and gazed
in silence at her. He
closed his eyes, and
then opened them,
asking, "How can
you go?"

"Come with me."

He nodded.

They walked out of
the oasis, across the
waste, and through a
fold to over there.

(Chaos. Order.

Lost.

Recalling:

A flame had
seared through
his eye. Over
that he tried to
go, and failed.
He sought a rock
or core within
himself, but only
found some sand.
Yet, he survived.

Now, he faced
this oasis. He felt
his love as shards
betrayed. His life
flamed fragments
of his memory.
All within that
tear of red.

other said as he
reached down
and turned the
pail downside
up. "You're lucky
there's no coin,
fool. I'll assume
you just forgot to
turn it."

The clown
dropped his head,
and so roughly
rubbed his face,
he smeared away
some paint.

The other
chuckled.

He groaned,
trying to find a
word to catch

                                            Antigone:

"Sans!"

    Oft the older man:

"Is that a woman heard by

me in time of want?"

                                       "Sans."

      "It is

         a woman.

Blessed

      gift of God

            to man.

Woman, can you hear?"

                                     "Aye!

                                       I hear

                                           and see."

"Come over

        here

            across to

me."

                                     "Aye. From

Chaos.

Order. Chaos.   Did God hug   the conscience
                       him?   of the man.
Order. Chaos. Order.

                       Did a love,   "Move along,"
Chaos. Order. Chaos.   personified, hug   the vested one
                                            ordered.

Chaos. Order. Chaos. Order.

Order. Chaos. Order. Order. Chaos.   The clown was
                                            silent.
Order. Chaos. Order. Chaos. Order. Chaos.

Order. Chaos. Order. Chaos. Order. Chaos. Order. Chaos.

Order. Chaos. Order. Chaos. Order. Chaos.

Chaos. Order. Chaos. Chaos. Order.

Chaos. Order. Chaos. Order.

Order. Chaos.

Order.)

the shattered child?   "Move along,"
                                            the man said
Or so inside, he asked, Did I respond?   without a grin.
With an arc of thought cascading into
reality, he imagined that some memory   The clown was

here to--?"

Oft the older man:
"Here,
       and
            over there
in time
      to press
           the petals
of your shape and feel."

Antigone:
"Sans!
      Where
           are you in
this my trial in shaping time?
So thus, I say, no!"

"No? So be it so.
Honor bound am I to not
do you on a no."

"I thank you,
           kind sir."

"You are most welcome."

within him asked, receding] to show
the woman on her feet. The child was in
another when and where beyond his ken
to grasp, and she had a single tear of red)
without a dream.

Parsafal opened his eyes.

A horse licked his face.

He chuckled, coughed and died.

(Chaos.

Order.)

silent, and
unmoving, still.

The other shoved
him as he kicked
the pail, yelling,
"Move along!"

Picking up the
rolling pail,
another clown
steadied

him from behind, and said, "Hold your ground, good fool!"

"Hard to hold what are only shifting sands," the first clown said,
taking the pail. "Maybe just a waste of time." He looked at the other
with a nod, and an already waning smile. "But thank you all the
same."

"That's hold enough for--."

The vested one pushed him, saying, "I'm only giving you one more
warning." But, he quickly backed away. "Move along!"

Antigone:

                     "Lecher

dishonorable

I mistook

        of you."

    Oft the older man:
"No,

        not of that school of thought   (Chaos.
am I. Loneliness   Order.
                                            Chaos. Order.)

long--."

                                          Sans:

                                     "Antigone!"

"That man!"

    Antigone:

                "Sans, over here, love!
Love."

      Sans:

            "Antigone."

Glancing for a moment behind him, the second clown said to the other one, "Along a winding wind's that way, my brother. Is your pail not worth a word or two?"

"And more!" He said, nervously watching their censor finger his badge. "I'd pale along beside you. So if you'd say that word or two, I'd play a jest for you."

"You catch my drifting thoughts as if you read them once upon a time."

"You're joking."

"Without knowing what to do--."

Grimly, the vested one interrupted, snarling, "Chaotic fools! I told you what to do. Move along!"

"About the rules," the second clown said in answer to him. "Move along about the laws to serve your foolishness. Laws and rules that stifle wit and art to only make some extra coin and folding just for power, and the few. Don't you see, art and story are like cheese, and your model insists all should be merely a yellow processed cheese food. Don't you miss a brie, or a gouda? Even cheddar? There's a difference in concinnity. The coin's derived from the story, not the other way around."

Oft the older man:
"Betrothed

       in passion

harsh and clear

       and dreadful

to behold in time;

a passing star

       in

joy and woe bestride a hope

of beauty into one

with truth: spiraling

stars, so intimate and in

wonder, Christ, the clown."

The censor retreated, saying, "stay back."

"Don't you see?" The first clown asked, reaching out to him. "Coin and folding can be gotten from any task or gift, but the poem and a story goes beyond such simple things. I do them. Take a little coin. I go. Simple."

The other spat at him, and snarled into his box, "Control?" He paused. "I have a developing wave." He backed farther away. "Here." Another pause followed as he began to circle them. "I'll need assistance." Looking about him now, he said, "That's right, and I have a cultural shock wave building up around me."

"Do you think he heard us?" The second clown asked.

"Not a word," the first one answered.

"Not another word, then. It's time to go!"

And so, the tale is told within the shadow an object hyperbole.

Postlude

""""Word by word, stone by stone, column by column.""
>   --First rule of reading, taken to be by some temple scribe,
>   Iraq, c. 4,000 B.C.E.

"'Word by word, scroll by scroll, column by column.'"
>   --First rule of reading, taken to be by some temple scribe,
>   Egypt, c. 3,000 B.C.E.

"'Word by word, page by page, column by column.'"
>   --First rule of reading, taken to be by some monastic scribe,
>   Italy, c. 900 C.E.

"'Word by word, scroll by scroll, column by column.'"
>   --First rule of reading, taken to be by some blogger, United
>   States, c. 2,000 C.E.

"'Word by word, page by page, column by column.'"
>   --First rule of reading, taken to be by some writer, United
>   states, c. 2,008 C.E.'

"'Here in this, one is free."
>   --First rule of reading, taken to be by some reader, United
>   States, c. 2,009 C.E.'"

"Here in this, one is free."
> --First rule of writing, taken to be by some scribe, United
> States, c. 2,013 C.E.

+